MW01534848

Layla, An Egyptian Woman

Fawzia Assaad

Translated by Melissa Marcus

The Red Sea Press, Inc.
Publishers & Distributors of Third World Books

P.O. Box 1892
Trenton, NJ 08607

RSP

P.O. Box 48
Asmara, ERITREA

The Red Sea Press, Inc.

Publishers & Distributors of Third World Books

P.O. Box 1892   **RSP**   P.O. Box 48

Trenton, NJ 08607   Asmara, ERITREA

Cover Art: Inji Ifflatoun
Cover Photo: Fadiah Haller-Assaad
Cover Design: Roger Dormann

Library of Congress Cataloging-in-Publication Data

Assaad, Fawzia.
  [Egyptienne. English]
  Layla, an Egyptian woman / Fawzia Assaad; translated by Melissa Marcus.
    p. cm.
  ISBN 1-56902-220-8 (cloth) -- ISBN 1-56902-221-6 (pbk.)
  I. Marcus, K. Melissa, 1956-   II. Title.
  PQ2661.S73E313 2004
  843'.914--dc22

                        2004021272

Preface

When I met Fawzia Assaad, she was teaching philosophy at the University of Cairo. That was in November of 1958. The city was mild, beautiful, noisy and colorful, in spite of the memories of the recent war, and in it floated an unrivaled fragrance: perfumes mixed with incense and amber, manure, honey and flowers. The air was soft.

Fawzia dragged me all the way to the ends of old alleyways, into houses decorated with ceramics, furnished according to ancient traditions, to sumptuous palaces, into mosques. She took me to the museum, she showed me, among innumerable marvels, the sculpture of Princess Nofret, made of painted limestone; she told me that her expression was that of the women of her race.

Later, I was introduced into the labyrinth leading to the Coptic church. I attended the Coptic mass, I followed my friend among the relics of the Coptic museum: embroidered fabrics, objects, inscriptions. Fawzia Assaad is a Copt. In order to tell the life of an Egyptian woman, she had to choose among many women, different in their origins, their way of life, their social status, their political and religious convictions. She elected Layla, who resembles her like a sister. And in reading the story of Layla, faithful to the traditions of her race, even though she is educated and liberated from the superstitions and prohibitions of her ancestors, I find the images of the past, glimpsed fifteen years ago.

She elected Layla, and through her, she has made the poetry of an outdated education, an intellectual and moral upbringing, understood by beautiful legends—Christian or dating from the epoch of the Pharaohs—come alive: because, she says, the Copts are the descendants of the ancient Egyptians.

But not only the past is to be found in Fawzia Assaad's book; there is the present, the dramas of the war, inner upheavals. There is the love of peace, desire, sometimes combats, the shame of defeats and the bitter joy of victories.

Fawzia Assaad says it: the Egyptians are not a warrior people; their still-indestructible irony allows them to remain lucid in the worst of moments, and to sometimes make fun of themselves. And the hope for calm and happy tomorrows does not leave them.

She doesn't forget her friends who died on the battlefields, or under bombs, nor those who spent years as political prisoners. She doesn't forget the efforts of those who fought in order to create a freer, more just society, who tried to help the poorest, to abolish privileges.

Coptic, and thus an element of a minority jealous of its sense of identity, attached to its traditions, proud of its ancestors, Fawzia Assaad wants above all to be Egyptian. She claims to belong to a great people who claim their varied roots from very ancient pasts, beyond which the future spreads—a possible future of peace, of prosperity, of gentleness—along the length of a great river where feluccas slowly glide.

The story of Layla the Egyptian is not a history book. Fawzia Assaad leaves to others the task of objectively telling—if that is possible—the events that have marked the past twenty years. She narrates not history, but a story, and the external events are seen only through the sensitivity of her heroine. This is what makes her tale so captivating. It is also what makes it familiar, fraternal, to us.

In ending, I would like to say how touching the tale of Layla's childhood was to me. In reading it, I discovered, to my surprise, that there were hardly any marked differences between the life of a little girl of Egypt and my own of times past. Layla's childhood, and my own, although they took place thousands of kilometers away from each other, nevertheless resemble each other. Is it because I, too, am Mediterranean? Or is it rather because children of all countries, through the disguises of customs and morals, nevertheless love, hate, fear, regret and dream in the same way?

Beyond the local color and change of scenery, Fawzia Assaad's tale is a kind of testimony that should serve to weave ties between worlds, to make a beautiful fabric of friendship, more sumptuous than the cloths, embroidered in the past by the Copts, that sleep in the depths of museums.

Suzanne Prou[1]
1975

---

[1] Suzanne Prou (1920–1995). Illustrious French writer. Her clear and precise writing, inspired by the Provençal light of the Mediterranean, still creates, in few words, the wonder of the novel's creative instant.

CHAPTER 1
In the Elysian Gardens of Cairo

"You are not an Egyptian."

This has been said to her a thousand times to wound her; this has been said a thousand times to flatter her.

And yet ...

What links her to Egypt dates back to the dawn of time. A patch of ground inherited from her ancestors roots her in a village of Upper Egypt, near places where, in days of old, people worshipped Heket, the Frog goddess, and Khnoum, the potter god with a ram's head.

Her color—the color of earth—identifies her with this land.

She is a Copt: a relic, a museum piece. She could serve as an example for an anthropology course.

"Look at this young lady; make her up in the style of the ancient Egyptians and you'll bring back to life the face of one of those women from the tomb of Nakht ... The same almond-shaped eyes, the same thick lips, the same low forehead ...

"Consider a reproduction of a mummy; then imagine this young lady dead, without make-up, without curly hair, without all of this flesh thickening the nape of her neck: aren't you struck by the resemblance?

"Turn your head, Madam, show us your profile. The skull is egg shaped: an egg leaning on its axis, the tip facing forward in place of the chin, the base flattened in back at the top of the head. The Akhenaten period accentuated this appearance.

"Permit me, Madam, to lower your bodice: the skeletal structure of the shoulders, the manner in which the bones overlap to

1

form a right angle, hardly rounded by the flesh, isn't it the same as in the paintings and statues of ancient Egypt?

"The Copts are the descendants of the ancient Egyptians, and the most striking proof we have of this is the incredible, profound similarity between their bodies, skulls and faces."

Friends told her that she resembled Lady Sennoui from the time of Sesostris the First, or that she resembled the wife of Ramses the Second. She copied the hairstyle of these women: a part down the middle, hair neither short nor too long cascading down her shoulders and back; but because it didn't curl enough, she wasn't able to fluff it up sufficiently to imitate the three-part wig. So, against her own wishes, she did her hair in a modern rather than an ancient style.

People remarked that the almond-shaped corners of her eyes were as low as Lady Sennoui's, and that her eyebrows were straight like Lady Sennoui's. She put on a lot of kohl to accentuate the resemblance to her ancient sister. But, unable to maintain the everlasting smile of statues, so much did she enjoy laughing and crying, she had to abandon the kohl, which ended up flowing onto her living face.

Her resemblance to numerous works of art didn't make her beautiful, because she was not a work of art.

But she felt "purebred," which, intellectually, meant nothing to her, but sentimentally inspired in her a certain pride combined with a shiver of death …

Egyptian: her ancestors were Egyptian, and so were the ancestors of her ancestors. As far back as one could trace her ancestry, there had been marriage only between blood relations (except maybe on her mother's side: one great grandmother, a "white Negress," a Greek woman—one small luxury, a trinket of foreign blood). If she lost track of her ancestry, she would recall ancient Egypt and would wonder: what did I do to survive so many centuries? Did my ancestors know how to love only people resembling them? Centuries and centuries of directed love have made me into an Egyptian woman proud to be an Egyptian.

The shiver of death lay in wait ...

In order to tell the story of "the Egyptian woman," one would have to tell a thousand, ten thousand, a hundred thousand stories, even more, as many as there are women in Egypt.

How would we choose among them? Which woman? The peasant, the city dweller, the petite bourgeoise, the rich woman, the poor woman? Or the one who, born rich, became poor, or the one who, born poor, became rich? The Egyptian woman who has not known how to liberate herself? The one who readily found freedom? The one who has never dreamed of it? The strong woman who controls her world, or the submissive object? Or the spoiled child who will never leave childhood behind? The woman who goes into the streets to demonstrate and is then locked up in political prisons? All of these, and many others are Egyptian women. We must, however, choose well.

This Egyptian woman grew up among women, all of whom were dressed in black: her mother mourning her father, her grandmother mourning her grandfather, Zebeida mourning her life ... And among a herd of boys—brothers, cousins, all of them at least four years older than she—who surrounded her with roughness and severity, tenderness and friendship, in a house with high ceilings, flooded by sunlight.

She was one of the very few girls who were wished for in this land of Egypt. Her parents had been captivated by the charm of another girl, their firstborn child. Like everyone else, they would have liked to have a boy to start with, for the name, for glory. A girl gives herself away, changes her name, whereas a boy prolongs the life of the father. And, too, a girl is such a source of worry until the day of her marriage (and she has to find someone to marry). As long as she has not changed her name, her father's honor hangs by a thread. If a young man courts her but doesn't marry her, her reputation and the family's honor are ruined. And then how can a husband be found? A girl carries no weight. Her mere existence humiliates her mother, who failed to bear a son.

When a son is born, the mother loses her first name (and the
first name is what has counted since the most ancient of times, what
determines for gods and men the existence of a human being). So,
when a boy is born to her, the mother loses her first name. She is no
longer called Zeinab, or Miriam, or Hanem; she becomes Om Farag
or Om Mohamed: Mother of Farag, Mother of Mohamed. But she
is not named Mother of a daughter; as long as she has not given birth
to a son, she stays herself, diminished, ill-loved, threatened with
divorce or abandonment.

But as for the son, he is named Ibn Ahmed, Ibn Daoud (the son
of Ahmed, the son of Daoud) and not Ibn Zeinab or Ibn Zebeida.

Thus her parents wanted a son. They had a girl, but a perfect
little girl. Then a boy was born on a day of riots, when the revolutionaries, fighting for independence, cried out "Yahia al watan! Long
live the country!" and got themselves killed by the English. And like
thousands of boys born on that day, her brother was named Yahia,
Long Live! And her mother became Om Yahia.

And her parents knew many years of happiness. They were rich,
they loved each other, and their children were beautiful.

The brother and sister had a Swiss governess who would not
allow the mother to interfere in their education. The mother permitted this and believed she was offering them the best of possible
worlds: Western refinement, French language from early childhood.
The governess was strict. Without a doubt, the little girl would have
liked to enjoy her mother's tenderness, but she only saw her for a half-
hour in the morning and on the nanny's day off. The little boy took
revenge for the governess's severity by playing a thousand tricks on
her, for which he was harshly punished. But the little girl was sweet
and obedient—too proud, incidentally, to accept punishments, and
besides, she had an intuition for good and evil. She was perfect:
beautiful and gracious, with a white complexion and black hair, and
always careful not to get her dress dirty. At the age of six she recited
poems and played the piano without feigning modesty or hitting
wrong notes, yet unpretentiously. She came into the drawing room
to greet her mother's friends with a curtsey and withdrew discreetly

after reciting her poem and singing her song.

"She was too beautiful for this earth." "She was not made to live." These words tell all: she was swept away by meningitis at the age of six. Her mother remained forever inconsolable.

The mother had to have another daughter. A son, only half welcome, was born to her. Finally, four years later, a girl came into the world, celebrated as no other girl had been on Egyptian earth, but in the strictest privacy, so as to avoid the evil eye that had caused the death of her older sister. The priest burned incense in the home. The aunts, uncles and older cousins offered the child many pieces of jewelry inlaid with turquoise to exorcise desire, carrier of the evil eye.

They called her Layla. They baptized her with no ceremony and no invitations. Three times she was immersed, completely naked, in the holy water of the baptismal fonts, in the name of the Father, the Son and the Holy Ghost, all the while shrieking with more energy than on the day of her birth.

The governess had left. Madam Morcos, the mother, could not forgive her for having stolen her first daughter's few brief years. Besides, Doctor Morcos had been appointed to another post in the country, and the oldest brother was studying Arabic in earnest in order to be accepted into the government schools. Other governesses passed through occasionally: the principle of their authority was henceforth contested, and strict discipline was rejected.

Layla was two years old when her father died. The family was already living in Cairo. Layla no longer remembered her father. He remained for her a portrait, framed in black wood, of a jolly generous man dressed in black.

He had left her to her mourning mother, to a family whose boundaries merged with those of the Coptic community. He had left her to innumerable substitute fathers.

She would have liked to remember the real man behind the jovial and generous portrait framed in black. What were you like? Mamma says you liked books and traveling. Would you have liked to see me with a book in my hand? Would you have allowed me to travel? What sort of ideas did you have about the education of girls?

Would you have forced me to marry at sixteen? At twenty?

Would you have given me to a boy with a promising future or to a rich boy? Or instead to a young man from an important family?

If you had been alive, Father, would I have been sought out by those "brilliant matches" who never did present themselves because there was neither a father nor a fortune to marry? I know it wasn't Mamma that you married, but my grandfather. You were lucky. But is it always so?

Other girls are worth more than I am: they have fathers. I have only uncles; it's not the same.

If you were living, Father, would we have returned to the provinces?

What kind of school would you have chosen for me?

And if it had been Mamma who had died, what then would my story have been?

It always seemed to Layla that the jovial, generous portrait smiled ironically when she would ask him these questions, and would remind her of his black suit and the black wooden frame. "I'm dead; so get your feet on the ground and look for another father. I'm in peace where I am."

Or Layla imagined him saying to her: "If I had been alive I would have forbidden you this intellectual affectation; I would have found you the husband you need."

This last image displeased her: "Mamma says that you liked books and traveling; you have an intelligent face. You would have been happy to discover that I too was intelligent, and you would have taught me what ideas were needed in order to change the world."

But the father was truly dead, and Layla's story began without him.

Three years after her father, Layla's maternal grandfather died, and with the small inheritance she received, Madam Morcos bought a piece of land so she could build the house that she would grow old in.

The inheritance was modest, and so was the land.

The family argued a lot. Layla's uncles set out to look for something they would find convenient, inexpensive, and respectable. The rich lived on Zamalek Island or in the Garden City neighborhood on the right bank of the Nile. Madam Morcos couldn't afford these places. She no longer wanted to live in the crowded middle-class neighborhood, Shubra, where her husband, before dying, had decided to have two large buildings put up.

Her brothers discovered another island for her, Al Rodah, or "Elysian Gardens." On Al Rodah there were pretty and modest villas surrounded by small European-style gardens. At the tip of the island there was even an abandoned palace, the Menasterli, surrounded by a small grove of mango trees. A large street separated the island into two parts, each bordered by a tight row of very unpretentious three- or four-story houses, yellow, gray or white. All kinds of businesses could be found there: the grocery store, the butcher shop, the dairy; and on the sidewalks, mountains of fresh fruits and vegetables from the produce farmers, and the poultry merchants with their cages full of pigeons, hens, rabbits; and in the road, the street merchants' carts. There was a lot of noise, a lot of life. Then there was a square and on the other side of the square an abandoned lot; then the street became silent, shaded, once again lined with modest villas, all the way to the uninhabited palace in its garden of mango trees.

A street lamp with two lanterns, one of which was broken, stood in the middle of the square.

Madam Morcos's brothers thought the place was perfect. They bought half of the abandoned lot next to the one-eyed street lamp (which they were supposed to have repaired but never did), and the construction of Layla's childhood home, which her mother wanted to be flooded with light, began.

The construction went on for a full year. One of Madam Morcos's brothers supervised the building site, as he would not have done for his own house, with the sense of honor that a brother in the East can feel, having accepted the role of the man in the family, in lieu of her dead husband.

Large rooms, verandas, washable walls, a beautiful wooden floor ... Madam Morcos's wishes were commands; her brother had the plans drawn up, brought in floor and paint samples.

While her brothers were in school, Layla went with her mother to see the progress at the building site. Disconnected images remain from these visits: workers who dug with shovels, filled straw baskets, and then poured out the contents of these baskets onto a mountain of earth. Layla never discovered where this mountain disappeared to. A foreman ordered around the workers and insulted them; he was the *rayes*, and he revolted Layla.

"He's mean," she would say.

"No, he's doing his job, he's paid for that."

One day when Layla saw the workers resting, assembled around a dish of squash with tomato sauce, she wanted to join them. They were breaking apart the bread, forming it into a shell, soaking it in the sauce and then scooping up a piece of squash. Then they would eat the bread and squash together without getting their fingers soiled. Layla grew up nostalgic about sitting in a circle of workers and peasants, breaking apart the bread with them, learning how to use it without getting her fingers greasy.

The hole in the ground changed shape; it became larger and larger, deeper and deeper. Layla's uncle was having a solid house built. Soon after, metal bars were planted in the ground and cement was poured. They saw the second floor take shape—where the family would live—then two more floors, which, rented out, would provide a regular income.

Should we build yet another floor? They argued: "Another floor means spending more money and you don't have very much," the uncles said. "I'll get some, I have my small jewelry," said Madam Morcos. She scraped around in the bottom of her drawer and sold her old jewelry by weight. (Could she have known that the "quaint" would become the "antique"?) What counted was that she wanted a fourth floor.

They joyfully moved into the house, with a feeling of security that Layla never found again. She had seen the deep foundations, the cement framework, and the solid thick walls. She and her family were at home; they were the masters, the owners.

Madam Morcos's house won her added respect. Upon the death of her husband, she could have taken refuge with her children at the home of one of her brothers, passed off all real responsibilities; the myth of feminine weakness granted her permission to do so. She had preferred independence, and this choice brought her greater credit.

A few years before, her marriage had allied two great families, equally old and respected. One family, her own, which had been settled for a long time in Lower Egypt, derived its prestige from the place that it occupied in the political scene of the period; the other family, from having owned land for a long time. The two families were full of respect for each other. After the death of Doctor Morcos, a sort of chivalrous jousting began between the families. For the brothers and brothers-in-law, the question was who would be the most solicitous toward Madam Morcos and her children. It was a matter of honor.

For her part, Madam Morcos jealously guarded her own honor. Out of fear that she would be accused of seeking to remarry or of having even the slightest desire to do so, she didn't permit herself any coquetry; not even a hint of make-up, not even a small white collar on her black dresses. In large Coptic families with imprecise boundaries, clans rather than families, mourning forever follows mourning. Madam Morcos didn't leave her state of mourning.

What a pity that white is not, in Egypt as in China, the color of mourning! In the Rodah house, white would have harmonized better with the light.

Madam Morcos never let the bitterness invading her heart show through in her words.

"It seems to me it was yesterday," she thought, "that I was young and beautiful; thirteen years have passed and I no longer have the right to be so."

She hadn't chosen her husband. One day her mother called her into the sitting room; a man whom she didn't know offered her a diamond bracelet. She recounts that she felt herself pale with anger and that she fled to her room ... But a few moments later she returned, hesitant. Hadn't she known for a long time that things would happen this way?

During all of her adolescence she had prepared her trousseau, had embroidered and adorned her delicate lingerie with lace and flounces. What did she talk about with her sister on those long afternoons when both of them plied their needles? They had hardly gone to school, hardly read. If not love, what could they talk about? Two sisters, two friends, one wise, the other crazy. One accepted the husband her parents had chosen for her, the other never married.

Madam Morcos's parents had grown up together, their families were related, and they had loved each other since childhood. They knew that marriages of love were the exception and that the matrons of the community, of whom several were keen matchmakers, were right when they said that love comes after marriage. But if one loves beforehand, what's the harm? And in fact, perhaps it's better that way. Madam Morcos's parents didn't rush things: they wanted to give love a chance.

Evening after evening, under the eye of the chaperon on duty (one of his future brothers-in-law) and with the blessing of all of society, which is satisfied for a while with unofficial engagements, Doctor Morcos courted her. Some good souls—they're always to be found—had warned him: his fiancée was in fragile health. Perhaps she even had tuberculosis. For a moment, he allowed himself to be troubled by these stories. What torture! And what a joy, on the other hand, to find a gracious and charming fiancée shining with health.

Doctor Morcos vowed great admiration to his future father-in-law. In his eyes, he was an important figure whose glory reflected on the entire Coptic community, both a man of experience whom Sultan Hussein had rightly honored, and a noble-hearted man. This admiration for the father naturally carried over to the daughter and turned into passionate love.

He showered his fiancée with gifts, and the latter measured her worth—for every young woman has a quoted worth—by their number and importance. But between the couple there were also looks, embarrassed laughter, and sometimes, accidentally, their hands met.

Had Madam Morcos's father wanted this marriage? Or was it only her mother? She worried about the three little sisters who wouldn't be able to marry before their older sister had done so. Now, the doctor had land, a medical practice, and a reputation for being a gentleman. Solid values. That being the case, what did it matter if he were neither a diplomat nor a chamberlain! Laying siege to her husband, endlessly buzzing in his ears, she knew how to give weight to these arguments, so much so that the father gave in. Sometimes Madam Morcos maintained that he gave in reluctantly: he did not, in fact, want to part with his daughter.

Then came the official engagement day, the *gabaniot*. A large tent with Persian designs was put up in the garden as an extension of the sitting rooms. Inside of it, separate seating areas had been arranged for the men, the married women and the girls. For the married women's language, often too risqué, was not at all suitable for young girls. In spite of the world war over there in Europe, and the necessity of covering the lights so as not to offer a target for the aggressiveness of the central European powers, the celebration was brilliant. There, young girls established a reputation for being beautiful or ugly, which was then weighed along with their fathers' social status and wealth. The quality of the guests, the dishes served, the fees of the dancers and the clowns were discussed for a long time.

After the *gabaniot*, Madam Morcos had the right to go out with her fiancé, to choose her furniture, her chandeliers, and her dishes. All of this, of course, as long as she was chaperoned by one of her brothers.

She often said about her marriage, which took place several months later, that "it resembled a fairy tale." Without a doubt out of esteem for her father, the Sultan Hussein had put at her disposal his gilded coach harnessed with twenty-four purebred horses. Even before the ceremony, the Sultana Melek had a voluminous sapphire, set with precious gems and made into a bracelet by foreign gold-smiths, delivered to her in a velvet box by messengers in ceremonial dress.

At the appointed time amidst the loud noise of rods and cymbals, the patriarch, heir to the rival pomp of Byzantium and Alexandria, arrived, followed by his cantors who were surrounded with a cloud of incense. While the hymns of the Coptic liturgy filled the house, the patriarch blessed the engagement rings of the bride and groom, joined their hands together, placed their heads together, adorned them with the royal sash of honor, and placed two crowns, set with precious stones, on their heads. He said to the bride: "You are the Church," and to the groom: "You are the Christ." He prayed a long time for the marriage of the King and Queen, Christ and the Church. Then he withdrew in all his majesty.

The gilded coach harnessed with its twenty-four horses, the guests' more modest coaches, and forty-eight musicians on horse-back, waited at the church door. With the drums preceding them, the procession traversed the streets of the city toward Abdin Palace, where the Sultan Hussein and his escort watched for the arrival of the bride from their balcony. The procession stopped, and the Sultan had large trays taken down on which innumerous glasses of flavored syrup were lined up in parallel rows: Syrup of marriage. Syrup of joy: the same word in Arabic means joy and marriage. The procession continued its path all the way to the large apartment that the doctor had decorated lovingly for his wife, and whose balcony was decked with banners. A few hours later after the last guest had gone, when only the bride, groom, and their close relatives remained in the apartment left in the state of ruin common to the aftermath of parties, the two families simulated a small war. There were scowls, hostile silence, and the hint of threatening gestures. The wedding night was about to begin. Now, the bride might perhaps not be a virgin, the fiancé impotent, and the families could truly become enemies. They parted without saying goodbye to each other.

The reconciliation did not take place before the next day when the doctor went for breakfast with his father-in-law, the latter smiling and apparently convinced of the happy outcome of the wedding night. (However, Madam Morcos had said to her daughter one day: "It's rare that anything happens on that night; you're too tired, you don't dare.")

Madam Morcos had married a rich and generous man. In order to please her, he had followed the customs of the people of Lower Egypt by offering her furniture, dishes and silverware. "I brought only my lingerie and a few dresses with me," she could say to her friends.

How things changed! Since her father belonged to the best of society, her friends, until her marriage, had been chosen largely from among the young women, usually of Turkish origin, of the Moslem aristocracy. From one day to the next, she now kept company only with Coptic doctors and their Coptic wives. She felt completely at ease in this new milieu where everyone immediately accepted her. But she nevertheless continued to set aside one day, the second Wednesday of each month, for her former friends whom she already missed. She created and faithfully maintained this tradition for years, thus keeping a link with her past life, until the day that her husband was transferred to the provinces. She would no longer see the friends of her youth.

The doctor died. Each time she passed the threshold of the house, where the deceased's portrait kept a watchful eye, Madam Morcos behaved as if an immense danger threatened her. A faceless danger with multiple faces. Anyone—a distant female relative, one of her husband's former patients, or even the beggar woman stretching out her hand at the church door—yes, anyone had the power to make her die of shame, to take away her dignity by insinuating in front of others, or, even worse, by persuading her, herself, that she was languishing away because she no longer made love. Madam Morcos is on the lookout for expressions which could suggest that she is as unworthy as a prostitute. She must not relax her vigilance for even an instant; she must not allow the slightest possibility for slander. Undoubtedly, her conduct is irreproachable, but that is not enough. Everything about her, from her unchanging black dresses to her eyes that never pause to look at a man, everything must say and even cry out: "I scorn what you call love. I will not sully myself. Marriage is not to be repeated."

Cousins lose their husbands and remarry. Rumors develop around her, reinforcing Madam Morcos's feelings of superiority. But time passes, and people sniggered and then forgot the very existence of the remarried cousins. In the same way, a few years later they will forget that Madam Morcos was once beautiful and virtuous.

Her house was large and welcoming, and the oldest of her brothers settled there to finish his days. Madam Morcos watched over him until his death.

The oldest brother was blind, suspicious, argumentative and jealous. His days were spent in a nightshirt, wandering from room to room; he seemed to have but one goal and one joy in life: to torment his sister. He went as far as throwing suspicion on the relations between her and her brothers-in-law! Too intelligent to believe his own accusations, he was nevertheless mean enough to enjoy himself in this game. For years he spilled his venom in daily doses, and this increased as age added to his infirmities.

Yet the children loved him. Had they perhaps come to discover the other side of his personality? On winter nights, they settled around him in the large sitting room as close as possible to the etched copper brazier, whose lid was shaped like an Egyptian minaret. They listened, enthralled, to his tales in which God and the Devil, one living in paradise and the other in hell, intervened quite naturally in the affairs of men. When the uncle was in a particularly good mood, he made a spectacle of himself: the palm of his hand on his left ear, he sang in tune, his voice barely quavering and sharp, hymns from the Coptic liturgy.

On Sunday, he put on his holiday suit and went to church to sing mass. Is the blind man a visionary as suggested by the Arabic language? Does custom demand that the cantor be blind, in the image of the harpist who plays in Nakht's tomb? The uncle sang, accompanying himself with cymbals, and he was sensitive to the rhythm rather than to the lyrics he had learned by heart. After which he was the first to receive communion, the first among the men, for the women here, as elsewhere, are separated from men. Supported by a choirboy, he would take off his shoes and cross the threshold of the iconostasis, followed at a distance by the respectful line of the other communicants. Three times the uncle went around the altar to receive the body of Christ, and three times again to drink the blood of Christ. Then with the help of the choirboy, he put his shoes back on and returned to his seat in silence.

Then came his moment of glory. He was the first among the group of men, the first to take his place on the reserved benches that face the mass of the faithful. He, the cantor, the blind man, the visionary, he had the privilege of being thoroughly sprinkled for a long time with holy water.

Always the first to leave, he would then go buy, at the door of the church, that good holy bread with its smell of yeast and the Coptic cross imprinted on its crust: a solid square cross, each end of which terminates in another cross, such that the twelve branches thus formed symbolize the twelve apostles and four times the Trinity.

After returning to the house, the blind uncle put his nightshirt back on and waited for lunch as he hummed church melodies. At the table, he again began making insinuations. But he especially saw to it that the children didn't spit out either orange or watermelon seeds, nor olive pits, for fear that they would at the same time spit out a crumb of Christ's body or a drop of Christ's blood.

A large staff of servants helped Madam Morcos take care of her big house, her little family and her blind brother: a porter, a gardener, a male nurse to look after or carry the uncle, an old cook, a young *soufragui* in a caftan of satin-finished cotton with bright colored stripes, to wait on them at mealtime. Some women, always dressed in black, because they wore Madam Morcos's old dresses, came regularly to renew the family's wardrobe or to re-cut old clothes. Other women, also dressed in black, like all the common women, did the weekly laundry. They would count the pieces of clothing, carry them onto the terrace, and wash them with great amounts of soapy water in round and flat tinned copper basins. They would then dry the clothes in the sun and bring them in when night fell, after having recounted them, which invariably drew them into noisy discussions, for the morning and evening numbers almost never matched.

Osta Sadek, the old cook, often got drunk by gulping down fuel alcohol for the *primus*, those noisy portable copper-plated stoves used at the time. Infuriated, Madam Morcos sent him away, and thinking that a woman cook would cause her fewer worries, she hired Zeinab. Until then the kitchen, where a man worked, had been a forbidden garden for Layla. Henceforth, she had the right to spend a good part of her days there.

At first sight, the arrival of Zeinab only added a new black silhouette to the black silhouettes already populating the house. However, after a closer look, one could see that the so-called austere dress was made of a transparent cloth trimmed with a gracious flounce and one could make out another dress, underneath, made of a flowered cotton fabric. It's true that, out of decency, Zeinab never took off her first protective dress in Madam Morcos's house. But the sparkle in her eyes, brought out even more so by kohl, revealed how much the other dress, the one she hid, could be gay and loud in private.

Like many other aged women, widowed or divorced, who no longer need fear a man's jealousy, Zeinab no longer wore a veil. However, her gaze was never fixed, and there was, one would have said, always something a bit secretive in it. Her eyes, whose expression she knew how to vary with quick movements of her pupils, had stayed those of a woman who wore the veil.

Zeinab worked little and prayed a lot: five times a day. Layla never saw anyone pray with such fervor. Her sleeves rolled up, Zeinab began by washing her hands three times, thanking Allah, the Powerful, the Merciful, for creating water for purification and instituting Islam, the light, the guide, the path to gardens of delight. Three times, too, she washed her mouth, then picked her teeth, and blew her nose forcefully as she pinched it between the thumb and forefinger of her left hand to help her get rid of its impurities ...

Methodically, diligently, she thus went through her ablutions, sometimes for more than a half-hour without ever ceasing to invoke the name of Allah. While washing her face, she asked him for the grace to whiten it on the day when the faces of the just will be whitened and those of the reprobates blackened. While washing her ears, she implored Allah to make her hear the good word, and while washing her feet, she begged him to help her stay on the right path and not allow her to falter.

Then the actual prayer began. Kneeling on a carefully unrolled mat, which she would quickly put away once her prayers were finished, for fear of any soiling, and facing toward Mecca, she bowed her forehead low to the ground, then got up, and again bowed low.

Sometimes Layla purified herself and prayed with her, as a game or perhaps out of fear of the hell about which Zeinab told her terrifying stories. With slight variations, they matched those of the blind uncle.

She was very unhappy when Madam Morcos sent Zeinab away. For a long time she believed that her mother had finally become tired of this cook who never stopped praying. She was mistaken. Because of her constant concern about tracking down any impurity, Zeinab (her mistress was the first to admit it) "did very clean cooking." Zeinab's sin was not prayer but love …

"Zeinab didn't do wrong," Madam Morcos later explained to her daughter. "But she was flirtatious. The porter, the gardener, the soufragui all fell for her. I sent them away. Then it was your big brother's turn: I had to get rid of Zeinab."

Layla never knew whether it was love, or the comedy of love, that was reprehensible. Zeinab disappeared from her life. She blended in with the mass of those women covered in black crêpe, whose whole baggage fits in a bundle; those women with an uncertain destiny, living day by day, in search of a roof over their heads or a way to survive.

Zebeida, the one whom Layla preferred among the women in black of her childhood, took Zeinab's place. "Let her come here," the uncle had said. And no one dreamed of contradicting a blind man.

Her bundle contained only two or three dresses, unrefined lingerie, and a rough *loofa* for bathing. She was then maybe forty years old. Little, a bit plump, her face round and delicate with tiny eyes that were already sick. One day her husband had taken a second wife. She couldn't tolerate it. She left him her two children and stopped veiling herself. Let her young rival decorate herself henceforth with the crocheted veil and the *arousa*.[1] As Zebeida was no longer the loved wife, she no longer had the right to do so.

For years, sometimes as a maid, sometimes a nursemaid, offering her masters all of the tenderness that she carried in her, Zebeida had looked for a home where she would be welcomed and loved. In vain.

She finally found it in the Morcos household. She dedicated all of her time to her new family, only isolating herself for brief prayers. She did the shopping, the cooking, and the dishes, walked little Layla and rested only in the evenings, when she would sit on the floor, legs crossed, at the foot of Madam Morcos's armchair.

Once a week, she would take a few hours off, leave the neighborhood and cross the Nile just for the pleasure of seeing once again the crowded streets of Old Cairo, forgetting herself in the bustle and heat of the crowds. Sometimes, for want of anything better to do, she would bargain for an earthenware jug or a bauble. But she never went near the places where she had loved and suffered in bygone days.

Sometimes she saw her ancestors in a dream. They told her they were hungry or that their souls were not in peace. When she awoke, she would then plan to go console them and feed them as quickly as possible. And the following Friday, she went all the way up to Qarafa, the cemetery of Old Cairo located at the very top of the city. Friday is the day that creation was finished, when Adam was born and entered paradise, and also the day when the hour of judgment will sound. On that day in the mosques the *imam* reads the sura of the cavern which announces the awakening of the dead, promising reprobates the torments of fire and molten bronze which burns up faces; promising to the righteous the gardens of Eden, the freshness of streams, clothes of silk and green brocade, and soft couches.

---

[1] A carved silver or copper cylinder worn coquettishly on the bridge of the nose.

Thus on Friday, Zebeida, like the women of Methuen's tomb, a basket of bread on her head and a jug of water in hand, would visit her ancestors. Did she hear from the depths of time the voice of Horus ordering offerings to be brought to Osiris's tomb?

"If I were rich," she said to Layla, "I would have a ram sacrificed for my ancestors."

But she had only water and bread to offer them. She would sit on the very earth covering them as she recited her prayers. Poor people surrounded her. Some had brought their ancestors a plate of *koschari*, a mixture of rice and lentils, or of *mefatta'ah*, a dessert made of nuts of all kinds cooked in molasses and melted butter. Zebeida broke her bread and shared everything with everyone. She chatted with her ancestors, talked about her ancestors: her mother, who had taught her dignity even in poverty; her father, a potter in the streets of Old Cairo, who had never dreamed of taking a second wife; her brother, carried off by cholera in the prime of life; her little sister, dead from typhus. She told of her life: the "daughter of evil" who had taken her husband from her, the evil eye which had destroyed everything.

She had one great worry: to marry off her daughter, who was fifteen years old at the time. She had gone from disappointment to disappointment with her son. At eighteen years of age he had gone straight from reformatory school to prison. But Gamila, whose name means "beautiful," and who resembled her name because she was as radiant as the moon on her fourteenth day, filled her with pride.

All of the money she earned in the Morcos household became solid gold jewels for Gamila. Zebeida was wise; she understood the order of things, she knew that a girl covered in gold attracts the eyes of men. For Gamila she wanted nothing else other than pure gold, because it was the best means, she thought, to make her be noticed by "a son of means" who would make her happy.

Gamila lived with her father, the owner of a bit of sidewalk and a beautiful pile of sweet-smelling fruit: guavas, mangos, melons, watermelons, figs. Starting at a very young age, she had helped to sell with her stepmother and her brother, and had learned early on how to play with her eyes and seduce. Was she going to marry soon? Zebeida was getting impatient.

"Our luck hasn't changed," she said, "my daughter is going to remain fallow."

"Patience, Zebeida," answered Madam Morcos. "After all, Gamila is only fifteen years old."

"That's the beautiful age, Madam; a flower is picked when it blossoms. Afterward, it fades and nobody wants it any longer."

"God is great, Zebeida, it is He who holds our destinies in his hand."

"What can one expect from a destiny like mine, Madam?"

And once again she repeated her litanies against her husband's young wife:

"That 'daughter of evil' has the evil eye. She's jealous of me and jealous of my daughter. Even though I left her the house and my husband, she still doesn't tolerate that he speaks of me with respect. Enough! One has only one's destiny."

The blind uncle died. Madam Morcos had cared for him, washed him, and carried him every time the personal nurse was away. She had put up with the sourness of a man who had seen only the dark side of life. She closed his eyes, dressed him, and placed him in his coffin. She received all the women who had quickly come to express their pain, and she fed them for three days.

Forty days after the uncle's death, Layla's grandmother took over.

An even darker black silhouette. The dresses of the newly arrived woman fell all the way to her ankles, whereas Madam Morcos's came only to the middle of her calf, allowing one to at least guess at the whiteness of her legs through her transparent silk stockings. Furthermore, contrary to the other women of the house who only hid their hair from strangers, the grandmother didn't take off, even in private, the black scarf tied around her head. Her serene white face, shrunken by deep wrinkles, left Layla forever with the memory of a luminous point of light piercing the darkness.

They called her Teta, from the name that the Turks give to their grandmothers, and which they had adopted because it sounded pleasant to the ear. Teta walked with difficulty, shuffling slowly from one foot to the other with the help of a chair that she pushed in front of her. At least she asked for no one's support, which gave her the illusion of independence. She had never been taught to read or to write, but she knew how to recognize numbers, and she never made mistakes in her accounts.

Teta had had her share of joy and pain: the joy of having married a man whom she loved and who gave her many children (her life had consisted of a series of pregnancies); the pain of bringing into the world a blind son, and much later, of seeing one of her daughters refuse all the suitors presented to her, rebelling more and more openly against her family and finally leaving for God knows where, abroad, where she was perhaps living in sin.

The departure of the rebel was followed almost immediately by the marriage of the two younger daughters who were only too happy, after so many years of waiting, to no longer be restricted by the custom which forbade them to marry before their older sister. And Teta found herself alone. Later on, Madam Morcos decided to take her into her home.

Layla was even more delighted about the arrival of her grandmother, because she would have the privilege of sharing with her the large bedroom, which was the most spacious and the brightest in the house.

There was a big commotion in the Morcos household while workmen moved the furniture all around. Finally, the bedroom was made up as a sitting room in the Trianon style, pale pink and pale blue. Pushed all the way to the end of the room, the grandmother's and granddaughter's beds were separated by a folding screen decorated with bows and flowered medallions. A portrait of Teta was placed above the wing chair; she was young, exquisite, her bust showing daringly in a very low-cut pink bodice decorated with rich black lace. On the opposite wall, next to a lamp similar to those formerly used in Saïs, was a picture of Saint George slaying the dragon and a cup filled with oil from which emerged a wick that burned day and night.

In the middle of the sitting room, on a square table, an alcohol-burning lamp, a coffeepot, cups and small dishes full of incense, amber and cardamom—all covered with a white cloth—had been placed. Every day around ten o'clock, Layla's uncles and the family doctor came for coffee, red tarbooshes on their heads; they wore white suits in the summer, blue, gray or chestnut in the winter, sometimes a black tie as a sign of mourning. They brought candy for Layla, or beautiful colored pencils, or a shining brand new silver coin.

The grandmother lifted off the cloth covering the utensils, measured the water, the sugar, and the coffee into the coffeepot; she kept an eye on the mixture on the fire, watched that the surface of the coffee would foam, thicken like cream and swell. Each person was served according to his taste: a little sugar, a lot of sugar or none at all, a piece of amber in the bottom of the cup, a pinch of cardamom.

Sometimes Madam Morcos's sisters would join their brothers. It was the moment for them to exercise their talents as clairvoyants. After drinking his coffee, one of the uncles held out his cup to them; they would turn it over nimbly onto the saucer, leaving the coffee grounds the time to spread out and form designs which the sisters interpreted, discovering in them portents of events wished for or feared.

Then Teta would wash the utensils in a basin of fresh water, put frankincense in the bottom of a dish, burn it, incense the cups and the coffeepot, arrange them and cover them again with the always impeccably white cloth. The uncles smoked a cigar and lavished advice on their sisters or their friends who had come to enjoy, as they had, the fragrance of the incense or the intimacy of the family circle.

For Layla, this coffee ceremony always remained one of the bright memories of her childhood. Later, when she went to school and no longer attended the coffee ceremony, she never failed, when she came home from school, to make sure that a smell of incense and cigars still floated in her room. She was never disappointed, and this gave her a feeling of security: day after day, her uncles continued to come for coffee and all of the family met there again, more united than ever.

With time, the cups and the coffeepot—which weren't worth anything anyway—chipped, but Teta didn't replace them: she loved them, she handled them slowly and with reverence, like a geisha presiding over the tea ceremony. But it wasn't a question of mere ritual: Teta served her children coffee with all of the love that a mother knows how to express in her most everyday gestures.

Madam Morcos and her family occupied only the ground floor, which gave her the right to the garden with its red wrought iron fence, covered with jasmine and bougainvillea. She had rented the upper floors to respectable families who were there to stay. On the fourth floor there had been a couple of moves in twenty years, but the fourth floor renters had never counted: Layla hardly knew them, they remained the strangers in the house. On the other hand, the renters on the third and second floors established their roots, one generation after the other, the daughter or the daughter-in-law taking the place of the mother in order to assure continuity.

A very dignified judge who lived on the third floor took the bus each morning to the Law Courts; he held one hand behind his back, his gait was slow and rhythmical, and he had a good-sized stomach. Each time he met Layla or her mother he would bow slightly, bring his hand to his forehead, then place it flat on his heart before putting it behind his back again and continuing on his way, imperturbable. He spoke little, he spoke well, like a judge. His wife: a black silhouette. At the time, their son was thin and shy. Since then he has increased in portliness and dignity. He takes the bus regularly to work, one hand behind his back, his gait slow and rhythmical, and his greetings courteous. He speaks little, he speaks well. Will he also be a judge? His wife is discreet and self-effacing. He also has a thin, shy son, which gives to this family an appearance of immortality.

Another Moslem family lived on the second floor, even more respectable because it could claim Turkish ancestry; even more respectable because Madam Hanafi had made the pilgrimage to Mecca. Mister Hanafi didn't seem less dignified than his neighbor the judge. It was a God-fearing family, an austere family.

But the little girl of the family always wanted to laugh, and in spite of her excellent training which demanded self-restraint, she often gave in to this desire. She was the same age as Layla, with a light complexion so valued in the Orient, and aquamarine eyes. Her name was Kawthar, from the name of a river in Paradise, sweeter than honey, whiter than milk, fresher than snow. She resembled her name.

The Hanafi family was traditional. Madam Hanafi didn't allow peddlers to knock on her door and Mister Hanafi forbade the young maid to go to the market: she could have allowed someone to murmur sweet nothings to her or have taken a few piastres from the family budget (it was never known which of these fears prevailed). Since they couldn't, after all, allow themselves to die of hunger, a wicker basket attached to a long rope came and went constantly between the balcony of the second floor and the courtyard of the house; it carried some change going down and came back up loaded with a pair of chickens or rabbits, a *ratl* of oranges or a watermelon.

The only inconvenient part of the system was that it left little room for the much-needed bargaining. Madam Hanafi had always missed the *mashrabeyya* of the ancient Arab houses, the carved wooden latticework placed over the windows so that the women could see out without being seen. Since she didn't have this convenience, she had made a rule for herself: her head must not go beyond the balcony railing, nor should the young maid's. They didn't see the merchants, were not seen by them, and had to raise their voices in order to be heard. How then could one buy a ratl of green beans at the right price or give a fig merchant, who had sold you a batch of rotten fruit, a piece of your mind?

The little girls were not allowed to visit each other. Set up at their windows on the side of the garden where big trees protected them from passing eyes, Kawthar and Layla used the wicker basket to walk their dolls from one floor to another, and to exchange colored pencils or messages.

During this time, from the courtyard side, Madam Hanafi, who was well hidden behind the balcony railing, watched the comings and goings of the neighborhood, noticed everything which seemed out of the ordinary, and peered into the interior of the houses, in hopes of discovering what went on in the hearts of others.

Every now and then, Madam Hanafi, Madam Morcos and other neighbor women, among whom several had made the pilgrimage to Mecca or to Jerusalem, paid courtesy visits to each other. They came back from these visits with a mass of the smallest details about how each one lived, which were then subject to all sorts of interpretations to be verified upon the next visit. Nothing concerning their female neighbors left these women indifferent: how much does Madam Atteyah's husband earn? And Madam Fadel's son, Hassan Effendi, an employee of the state? Why isn't little Farahat married yet? Their curiosity was insatiable and definitely indiscreet, but it also expressed all of the attachment—one would have to say love— that they felt for their neighborhood and their neighbors.

Layla's day began at dawn with the first bird songs and the first calls for charity from the legless cripple.

One could recognize the voices of the thrush in January, the hoopoe and the *bolbol*, the joyful nightingale of Egypt, in February, and the chaffinch in March. During the month of May, the chorus of birds was at its glorious height. The cripple sang his successive laments in his bass baritone voice: "God," he said, "You know our condition. Grant us success." From time to time, one would hear the tinkling of small change falling from a balcony to the sidewalk; then the lament, beautiful and monotonous, would begin again, accompanied by the chorus of birds amidst the silence of the still sleeping streets, and the dazzling sight of dawn.

The *ful medammes*[2] merchant had just set up—on the square below the one-eyed street lamp—his large smoking urn full of fava beans that had been steaming for the entire night. The servants and the common people of the neighborhood had themselves served large bowlfuls. Sometimes Zebeida joined them, for the family was wild about fava beans for breakfast. Each one savored them in his own fashion: cooked in butter with a beautiful fried egg in the middle, or mashed with goat cheese, or yet again seasoned with olive oil and lemon juice, or simply stripped of their skins and served with a touch of salt.

After breakfast the adventure of the market began. The ped-

[2] Stewed fava beans.

dlers knocked on the kitchen door, debated the price of a *wekkah* of zucchinis with Zebeida, of a watermelon or a mango. Then Madam Morcos would suddenly appear; she would feel a zucchini: is it hard? Slightly hairy? With her index finger bent back, she lightly tapped the skin of a watermelon: is the sound nicely hollow and deep? She reduced the price offered by Zebeida. The merchant swore he would lose money, lost his temper, left, and then returned.

"Tell Madam that I need this money to buy medicine for my sick little girl. I'll give her two kilos for five little piastres."

Zebeida would transmit the new offer to Madam Morcos and return with the implacable response:

"Madam says: not one more piastre. God will give you something."

It took even longer to buy a pair of chickens, because it was necessary to go all the way to the marketplace. Zebeida would hold the two robust fowls by the wings, finger them, and listen to their cackling; Madam Morcos felt their crop.

"There's a ratl of corn. All cheaters. They'd like to sell the wekkah of corn at the price of the wekkah of chicken. Do they take me for an idiot?"

Market, cooking, housework: all morning long, an intense effort was exerted in the big house. Layla, who liked this feverishness, would gladly linger in the kitchen, where she would follow, as if attending a performance, the newly developing events in the bargaining. But in her room, gathered around the grandmother, were the aunts, the female cousins and the friends, who chatted quietly without lifting their eyes from their tapestry-work or their crocheting; and Layla liked to embroider nearby while listening to their stories.

The afternoon nap allowed Layla to daydream in a house that had dozed off; they closed the blinds to be protected from the heat and light in the summer, from the light only in winter, and everyone slept soundly, as if in the middle of the night. The movement in the street stopped. The stores closed. The entire city slept. Upon awakening, they would refresh themselves: mango syrup, carob or sugar cane juice. Madam Morcos did her accounts and began to prepare for the next day; the aunts, cousins and friends began again their fancywork. The grandmother was still sleeping. Layla would go walking with Zebeida.

After they'd barely passed by the one-eyed street lamp, the adventure would begin: life, the heat of the street, the smell of jasmine in the springtime, the whiffs of grilled corn all summer long, the odor of mangos in September. Maybe Karagheuz, the Egyptian puppet character, would give his marionette show.

Zebeida was at home in the street. She would greet the shop owners on her way, make a friendly sign to the *chaouiche*, the neighborhood policeman, stop to gossip with the other women in black. She gave Layla a pair of rabbits to carry by their ears, or chickens to hold under the wings; or in order to please her, at the dairyman's she would let Layla place the order by herself, the smooth yogurts layered with cream that they would eat the next day. When they had to pass in front of a café, Zebeida would envelop herself even more tightly in her large black sheet and charge straight ahead, as she dragged along Layla. On the other hand, when she approached the Karakol (the police headquarters), she slowed down her pace. However, there were men there too. But the show was permanent at the Karakol, and Zebeida always hoped she could exercise her talents as a litigant.

Had a little boy spirited away a passerby's wallet, or pulled off the hubcap of a car? Had two cabdrivers whipped each other? It was an immediate opportunity for Zebeida to mix in with the passionate crowd, take sides, get worked up for the good cause and, if need be, testify, quote, challenge the facts; show to what degree, as a true daughter of her neighborhood, she knew its twists and turns.

Sometimes she attacked the guilty, or those presumed so: "Fear hell," she said to one, "or God will curse you." "Dog," she said to another, "if you don't fear the fires of Hell, God will never bless you." Layla was very proud of Zebeida's intimacy with God.

After they'd passed by the Karakol, they had to cross the Abbas Bridge. Two minutes would have sufficed, but Zebeida and Layla always dawdled. On celebration days, joyful groups of girls dressed in loud colors—canary yellow, candy pink, pistachio green—paraded

carts, singing, laughing and clapping their hands. In
y on the Abbas Bridge was a celebration day for Layla.
v a young bride en route to her husband's house. Then
Zebeida would do the inventory of the trousseau transported on
carts: the table, the dining room chairs, the sideboard, two side-
boards!

"The father of the bride," said Zebeida, "is rich and generous."

Women followed the procession. With a rapid movement of
their tongues, they yelled out cries of joy, *zaghareets*, resembling
those of birds of prey. Zebeida always joined in with the chorus of
zaghareets. On the Abbas Bridge there were also the horses, the
cabs, the drivers, the donkeys, the long silent processions behind
the coffin bearers. If the coffin has a tarboosh on top of it, a man has
just died; if the coffin has been covered with white flowers, it's a
girl.

How can one hurry when crossing the Abbas Bridge!

On the other side of the bridge, Layla and Zebeida rested on the
sparse grass of the tolerably dusty banks of the Nile. They mixed in
with the groups of women wrapped in their black sheets, sitting
like as many statue-blocks who have miraculously come to life, next
to their earthenware jugs full of water. Children in *galabiyyas* bit
hungrily into their bread, Layla ate her sandwiches and Zebeida
allowed her to spend her pocket money for peanuts, watermelon
seeds, sweet potatoes or grilled corn, jasmine necklaces ... There
were as many temptations. The licorice syrup merchant, with his
big jar worn across his body, wearing a turban and dressed as in
ancient engravings in a fitted vest and puffy-legged pants, played his
copper bowls like castanets.

Unfortunately, there were also beggars: the blind man, the half-
man in his wheeled cart made of an old crate, the exhausted young
woman nursing a baby with eyes full of black flies. No one said to
Layla: "If these people here are poor, it's because they don't work,"
or else: "Do you know that the beggars own half the country?" There
was no one to help ease Layla's conscience.

Sometimes, at the corner of a street or on the bridge or on a wharf, they would meet the Master of Antics with his monkey disguised as a clown. The monkey would greet them or else walk on his front paws and everyone would laugh until they were out of breath. Imperturbable, dressed in rags, the Master of Antics would wait for the spectators' money and bravos. Coins would rain down around him.

"One more time! Master, it was so funny."

Dressed as a bride, the monkey paraded around on the back of a donkey, and the people would laugh even harder. Sometimes, in addition to the monkey and the donkey, there was a child, a goat and a dog, also destined to become clowns. The more clowns there were, the larger the circle of spectators became.

"Master, you have an unusual little dog. By what miracle of balance does he hold himself, with his four paws placed together, all the way at the top of this scaffolding made of cubes? It's that you've learned to train him, Master: if he falls or if the cubes tumble down, you'll whip him; if everything goes well, he'll have the right to another piece of sugar. Of course he's scared, but the more scared he is the funnier it is. I congratulate you, Master."

"Master, you have many emulators in this world, who give out, like you, whippings and pieces of sugar. On the one hand, prison, humiliation, fear; on the other hand, empty words, vain promises. Entire populations serve them alternately, as clowns and then as spectators. Or at the same time as spectators and clowns ..."

In the evening after her bath, Zebeida told Layla stories about demons:

"Once upon a time there was a very powerful devil. His name was Gann Ibn Gann. He had a lot of servants, genies like him. He was very strong. He could carry enormous stones. He built the Great Pyramid with his servants. You're going to ask me why. To live there, by Jove! These sons of evil needed a big black hole. They're made of fire, you know. I've never gone into the Great Pyramid. It's all black inside. I've always been afraid that I'd see a genie come out of it."

And frightened, Zebeida would strike her chest.

"But what bad thing do these demons do?" asked Layla.

"They ride you like a horse and never let you live in peace."

"What do they look like?"

"I don't know. Like flames maybe."

"And ghouls, Zebeida, you told me they're devils in disguise. What does a ghoul look like? Act like a ghoul, Zebeida, act like a ghoul."

"Ghrrr, ghrrr!" cried out Zebeida, pretending to devour Layla, just like the wolf devoured Little Red Riding Hood. Layla liked this ghoul, her familiar wolf, a harmless monster, there to give little girls the shivers just for the pleasure of the shivers.

Sometimes Madam Morcos also told Layla a story:

"Once upon a time there was a man whom God wanted to test. He asked him to sacrifice his only son, Isaac, whom he had had with Sarah. Abraham took his only son, wood for a stake, a big knife, and he left ..."

Layla cried but didn't miss one word of the story; she never allowed her mother the slightest variation or allowed her to leave anything out.

On the second floor, Madam Hanafi told Kawthar the same story:

"Once upon a time there was a man named Abraham whom God wanted to test. He asked him to sacrifice his only son, Ishmael, the son of Agar. Abraham took his only son, wood for the stake, a big knife, and he left ..."

And Kawthar cried many tears; without getting tired of it, she listened to the story that her mother told her for the hundredth time. She would allow nothing to be left out nor any variation in the story.

The following morning, as the willow basket continued its comings and goings from one floor to the other, with its usual cargo of dolls and baubles, Layla and Kawthar would tell each other the stories of devils and the good God that they had heard the night before. The stories of genies matched well enough, but the one about Abraham and his only son left them puzzled: which of the two mothers was right? Was it Ishmael or Isaac?

Nevertheless, there was an area of understanding between the two little girls: in the two versions, the story ended in the same way with the sacrifice of the lamb which God, at the very last moment, had substituted for Abraham's son. A happy ending.

 In Egypt, too, the lamb is a part of all festivals and all celebrations: Easter Monday, for example, or the day of the Eid el Kebir, the smell of roast lamb would permeate the entire neighborhood of Rodah, for at the back of each garden, threaded onto a spit, they turned slowly, coated with melted butter and licked by the blue flame of burning coal.

On the occasion of the great Moslem celebration, Kawthar and Layla attended, as Isaac did in times past (or Ishmael), the sacrifice of the lamb. It happened at the very door of the house. They would put the lamb on its back on the ground and, with a big well-sharpened knife, the butcher would slit its neck in the name of God, The Compassionate One, The Merciful One. He would remove the skin from the carcass, gather a good quantity of blood in a tub, and spread the rest in the courtyard of the house.

Layla and Kawthar cried out of pity for the beast! But the courtyard would be washed down with water, and the two little girls would once again play hopscotch or knucklebones, quickly forgetting that the blood of a sacrifice had just been spilled. They never played for more than a half-hour because of the great displeasure that Madam Hanafi and Madam Morcos felt at seeing their girls in a courtyard.

How is it that these two women, in spite of everything, allowed these games? Madam Hanafi was Turkish, and what is more, Circassian. Now, Madam Morcos had the greatest respect for Turkish women and particularly for Circassians, who were known for their white skin and their beauty. For her part, Madam Morcos carried a famous name, that of her father. Now, famous names inspired the greatest respect in Madam Hanafi. So this is why the two women had allowed Kawthar and Layla to use the willow basket in order to exchange their dolls, and sometimes, to play ball for a whole half-hour, hopscotch, or knucklebones in the courtyard of the house.

CHAPTER 2

A Colonial Education

Madam Morcos wanted to give her daughter a careful education. The stakes were important: like every Copt, Layla was tied to the whole of the community, from the poorest to the most powerful, by distant relationship. Her education alone would determine which cousins' names she could use, which sort of marriage she could hope for, in which milieu she would be invited.

Madam Morcos's confusion was understandable. For a long time, like Mark Twain's mother, she refrained from sending her little girl to school. Layla learned to count with coffee beans, to read with a game made of letters cut from cardboard; she raised silk worms, feeding them with mulberry tree leaves that she would harvest during botanical expeditions to the Japanese garden of Hilwan or the banks of the Nile.

Madam Morcos taught all of this to Layla in French, for it was in French that she herself, as an Egyptian woman from an important family, destined to put up a good show in Cairo's salons, had learned everything, from her earliest days.

It wasn't the first time that great Coptic families thus found themselves torn between two cultures. Their history goes back to Hellenic Egypt; at that time, the feudal lords had adopted Greek culture, whereas the toiling masses had access to neither Greek nor power ... Until the day when the Greeks, driven back, brought back all of their nationals, including the Hellenized Copts with their goods and their culture, thus most likely establishing the moment in history when the cultural community prevailed over its roots.

Greek culture having sunk into oblivion, it was that of the West, after an interlude of a few centuries, that took over. When Layla was being educated, it was considered good form for a girl to know English or French perfectly, and preferably, both.

Let's make it clear: it wasn't a matter of preparing her for the direct exercise of power, but of making sure that she could one day marry someone who would hold or reach a position of power. The latter would have to also master Arabic culture, but like all the women of her milieu, Layla was excused from this.

However, upon the death of the doctor, Madam Morcos had learned, at her own expense, that social veneer is not sufficient for someone in charge of a family. Financial management, daily conflicts, the explanations owed to the suspicious civil servants of the tutoring service; all of this was done, not in the language of the salons, but in Arabic.

Thus Madam Morcos knew that this language, not needed for a spoiled and protected girl, would be necessary for her daughter. Because of this, the choice of a school posed a problem. While Layla watched her silk worms weave their cocoons, Madam Morcos mulled over her decision for a long time.

There was a Coptic school in Cairo where girls were taught Arabic and orthodoxy. Layla was sent there. She learned Arabic well, but to the great despair of her mother, she forgot French, acquired bad manners and enriched her vocabulary with some vulgar expressions. She was moving away from the model of her dead sister.

For a few months Madam Morcos tried to require her daughter to speak French. But Layla was not happy. Could they impose on her, like a starched and spotless dress, artificial speech that neither Zebeida nor the students at the school knew? Discouraged by the idea of letting her sink into the drab depths of the lower middle class, her mother finally took Layla out of the school and reversed the procedure: henceforth, she would be taught Arabic at home and French at school.

From her time at the Coptic school, Layla kept the memory of having lived for a few months in a crowded compartment; nothing but girls in the same uniform, nothing but Copts, like dogs in a kennel and hens in a hen house. A compartment for little Coptic girls.

After more thought, Madam Morcos decided, in return for great sacrifices, to send her to the Mother of God Boarding House, whose worldly mission in Cairo was to educate the daughters of the royal house and the Moslem upper middle class. Its spiritual mission was to assist the Jesuit order in its project of political control over men in high places, thanks to a Catholic, apostolic and Roman education.

A portrait ruled over Layla's education: that of her maternal grandfather, framed by silk embroidered with roses using a satin stitch, in a gilded wood frame. It sat imposingly in the living room, whereas her father's, framed in black, remained in the large entryway of the house.

People spoke little of her father to Layla, but a lot about her grandfather whose portrait was everywhere: one painted by Mahmoud Saïd, a great Egyptian painter, was in her uncle's office; he was also in the photo albums of all the related families, his tarboosh on his head as if he were a true Turkish pasha, his stiff bust under its armor of medals. Everywhere, he resembled the portrait in Madam Morcos's living room, with his bushy eyebrows, his thick mustache, his fearsome and arrogant look.

When Layla looked, in particular, at the photos of his state funeral, she would imagine seeing him through the coffin, carried on a gun carriage, and pushing away the worms who attacked his decomposing flesh with only the dignity of his eyebrows and mustache.

He looked at her from everywhere, and seemed to be saying: "You must be worthy of me. You must know how to carry my name!" And yet she didn't carry his name. She remembered little of him, and only through this portrait that haunted her childhood.

"An upright man," her mother told her over and over again, "of great and ferocious integrity."

Ferocious. Layla clung to this word that went so well with the eyebrows, the bushy mustache and the severe eyes.

His political career? "Court organizer in Upper Egypt, adviser to the Joint Appellate Court, then Finance Minister. The Copts have

Colonial – Private
Privilye   34   Schools

always taken care of finances, as if they were the Jews of the country. Very good people, the Jews, intelligent, hard working; like us, they're attached to the religion of their ancestors. But they're stronger, for they have a sense of solidarity that we don't have: the Copts shoot themselves in the foot … Your grandfather was a good Finance Minister. He taught us order in business and in life. May God have mercy on his soul!"

"If he'd had enough money," continued Madam Morcos, "he would have given me an education, as he did for my brothers. But he was an upright man; he had only his salary. He used the fifty feddans[1] given to him for translating the Napoleonic Code, he sold them in order to have a sumptuous villa built for us. He would have done better to think of our education. The boys had glory, and the girls had marriage. Each person lives according to his time.

"He was Prime Minister during difficult times, when the Wafd[2] was fighting for independence. The revolutionary leaders were exiled to the Seychelles: Saad Zaghloul, Sinot Hanna, who sold the diamond that he wore on his hand in order to feed his comrades, and many others, too. Blood flowed in the streets, the rioters were trampled. Your grandfather had the courage to take the reins of government. He wanted to negotiate; send the English home peacefully. The revolutionaries wanted to wage war. 'With old slippers?' he asked. He was accused of treason. They gave a Copt named Al Eryan the job of assassinating him. Your grandfather was riding in his official carriage, harnessed with two horses, his four motorcyclists in front. Al Eryan shot his revolver. Fortunately, he aimed badly; the bullet lodged itself in a tree trunk…

"Another Coptic Prime Minister, Boutros-Ghali, was assassinated. It was at the time of joint courts: the foreigners were the masters, the Egyptians the slaves. In Denchway, an Englishman who was duck hunting had killed a woman. The woman's son took justice in his own hands and killed the hunter. Boutros-Ghali led the inquiry with Lord Cromer. He signed the order to hang four innocent men, to have all the men of the village whipped, to humiliate an entire people. All of that in order to avenge the death of a single Englishman.

[1] Feddan: five feddans equals 2.2 hectares.
[2] Wafd: a delegation sent to negotiate independence from English rule. The word indicates a revolutionary movement of the nineteen twenties.

Al-Wardani killed Boutros-Ghali."

In the past, after Doctor Morcos had settled in Benhah, Al Eryan's family lived there, too. Madam Al Eryan sent a woman messenger to Madam Morcos to ask her permission to pay her a visit. Madam Morcos hesitated for a long time: admittedly, her father had pardoned the author of the assassination attempt, but could she forgive him? Her husband concluded:

"It was a political affair among Copts," he said. "I don't want you to be on bad terms with someone in the city where I work."

So Madam Al Eryan paid a visit to Madam Morcos. They drank syrup-sweetened drinks, ate candied dates stuffed with almonds. The question of the failed assassination then came up.

"You understand," said Madam Al Eryan, "it had to be a Copt. In order to avoid a religious war ..."

"Let us speak of it no more," said Madam Morcos. "It's a political matter that doesn't concern women."

She never returned this visit; it was her way to leave politics to the men.

Yet the doctor had tried to explain the art of politics to his wife. In the library, Layla had discovered a book by Machiavelli that was covered with her father's hand-written notes. He had underlined these sentences: "Every time a powerful foreigner comes into a country, all of the weakest in that country unite for the new arrival, for they are jealous of yesterday's rulers. And the invader doesn't have to worry too much about winning them to his cause, for they immediately join forces with him; he needs only to be careful of giving them too much power."

And in the margins the doctor had noted: "The Copts have always been suspicious of foreigners. The greatest among them have assimilated the culture of the occupying forces only in order to better defend their identity and preserve their roots. When one among them gave the impression that he was collaborating with the foreigner, he always found another Copt in his path who'd been delegated by the whole community to shoot him."

Every time Madam Morcos spoke to Layla about her grandfather, Layla looked for the portrait of her father and those brilliant eyes, so open to the future. She would have liked to have him framed in light, rather than in black wood. But when she asked her mother to talk to her about her father, Madam Morcos sighed and shrugged her shoulders:

"A fine man," she would say, "may God have his soul. He used to say to the one-eyed man: 'You are one-eyed.' I told him: 'It isn't good to tell all.' He responded: 'One must always tell the truth.' We didn't understand each other."

The doctor was a direct descendant of the Saïd, the peasant land of Upper Egypt; his father was rich. He had gone to Cairo to study medicine; he had learned English as a foreign language, because medical studies were done in English. Then he had married into a well-known family, a father-in-law, a lifestyle.

Layla's grandmother didn't know how to read or write; she spoke neither French nor English. It was different for Layla: Europe was the fashion. The ways of the occupying forces were important and desirable. Layla's career was marriage; it had to be secured.

Layla learned the history of France in books that got bigger with the years, and whose pictures gave way to concise writing. She learned by heart the list of French departments and their towns. She acquired a solid knowledge of French literature, from the epic poems to Zola. She grew up in sweet ignorance of Egyptian history, geography and literature.

Just like the young French girls raised in the convent, she learned that when you walk two abreast, the devil is there in between; he is there when you look at yourself naked in a mirror or when taking a bath; and there, too, with the little schoolboys climbing the garden wall, the handsome young men encountered in the street who make you dream of your cousins, maybe even your brothers …

Man and the devil were one and the same. She was sheltered and safe at the boarding school, but one had to learn to arm oneself, to be strong in order to confront the world of vice. Or she could be even stronger and stay in the boarding school, become Christ's fiancée and live protected from the devil until death.

As far as religion was concerned, Layla learned what she was taught: pages of the Gospel by heart, catechism, and how one could commit a sin through thought, action or omission. As for the Pope's infallibility, her aunts and her mother didn't believe in that; it was necessary that Mary, mother of Christ, give the lessons on that issue. As for knowing whether it was proper to speak of Christ's *natures* or of *the* nature of Christ—human and divine—they didn't even suspect that it was a controversial doctrine. Mary, mother of Christ herself didn't know anything about it.

And yet there was so much blood! During the sixth century the patriarch Apollinaire threatened the Copts, falling prey to Jacobite heresy: "I fear greatly for you that the emperor will send your wives into debauchery and make orphans of your children." They threw rocks at him, but he had the faithful massacred.

The Catholics had no more soldiers, but they could send their fellow man to hell. From the top of his pulpit, the chaplain thundered: "Whoever does not follow Peter and his Church will be condemned to the eternal flames. Satan tried to make this beautiful country of Egypt, evangelized by Saint Mark, fall into the darkness of heresy. Do not go to the orthodox church. Pray in your homes on Sundays rather than celebrate mass with the heretics."

Coptic adolescent girls, tormented by the fear of hell, went against the will of their parents and converted, sometimes secretly. Later they would marry in the orthodox church, and if they wanted to divorce, they would take out their Catholic certificate of baptism from the bottom of a drawer and obtain absolution from the Roman Church for countless years of "cohabitation." All of this shocked the young Moslems who didn't have need of such hypocrisy in order to get a divorce.

"Layla, Egypt is used to these things," her uncle told her one day. "After Osiris's paradise, the Pharoahs instituted the paradise of the sun, where only they alone were admitted in the solar Barque. When the Pharaohs of the sixth dynasty became poor and needed the rich, they established a nobility with a right to eternity. Paradise was slowly democratized, but it did not become a civil right until after Akhenaten and the wars between the priests of Amon and the followers of Aton. We must hope that, one day, the right to enter paradise will become universal ..."

Because she was orthodox, one Sunday out of two Layla was excused from mass at school, to the great regret of the nuns.

She and Madam Morcos cut through the small back streets in the direction of the bridge that separated their Elysian Gardens from the poor neighborhoods. There was a strong bridge quite strangely named "the bridge of the just king." Was its role to better unite or to better separate the rich from the destitute? Like the arm of the Nile which it spanned, it was a very modest bridge, and it didn't even open to the feluccas as did the Abbas Bridge on the other side of the island. A cloud of dust extended it all the way through Old Cairo, up its unpaved streets.

Before sinking into the haze of dust raised by the pedestrians, the donkeys and the carts, Layla would look for a last bastion of greenery, a thousand year old banyan tree whose trunk, people said, housed an old woman with her bundle, her gas stove and her pots. In spite of her curiosity, Layla had never caught a glimpse of her.

Layla and Madam Morcos moved through a crowd in which all of the feminine silhouettes reminded Layla of Zebeida. They walked between faded façades of buildings, amongst heaps of earthenware, pieces of pottery, and arrived in front of the El Amr mosque, at Saint George Church, sumptuous, gleaming, and arrogant, with its cross on top of a dome and its rooster perched at the top of a tower.

A door made of huge beams, and fitted with an enormous wooden bolt, had once shut in a subterranean city where the Copts took refuge from massacres. After going through this door, which at the time was not yet blocked by a pile of dust, they entered a network of winding alleys with low ceilings bordered by houses with carved wooden balconies, and decorated with lanterns placed on top of crosses. The mother and daughter went down a staircase to the Abou Sarga church and even lower, toward the crypt that was flooded when the water of the Nile rose, and where, according to legend, the Virgin and baby Jesus rested during their flight from Egypt.

They meditated for a moment, before going back upstairs to the nave reserved for the women, where each one, in the heat of the crowd, seemed to be waiting for the Almighty Father, the Savior. Layla could read in their faces the stillness of centuries. She imagined that, upstairs, the huge door of patinated wood closed slowly, inexorably; she waited for the big primitive bolt to slam shut ...

There was, indeed, above Abou Sarga and beyond the old door, a church that one could reach by means of a large staircase: Mo'allaga, the Suspended One, with its glorious icons. But Madam Morcos only went there on celebration days or for marriages. Otherwise, she had a secret and mystical penchant for subterranean churches, where the vivid memory of the first Christians and the persecutions they were subjected to, lives on. What force did she want to draw from there?

Kawthar went to a government school. She was off on Friday, Layla on Sunday. They were growing up with the look of modesty characteristic of traditionally pious people. Their different educations progressively separated them, as they would separate Layla's two brothers: one going to government schools, the other, the younger brother, to those of the Jesuits.

Every Friday a sheik came to teach Kawthar the Koran, with all of the exactitude imposed by Islam. Since the day that he had pushed her into a corner and made her aware of his sexual desires, Layla detested running into him in the stairwell. Had he also tried with Kawthar? Layla never dared speak of it. The Coptic priest, who was always trying to negotiate marriages—in return for money!—didn't inspire in her any more confidence than did the sheik.

Kawthar and Layla played together less and less often, and thus Layla became very sad. School deprived her of the warmth and security of the house. At the beginning, she turned pale at the idea of returning there; her mother spoke with the nuns who then deigned to adorn their austerity with a thin smile.

"If you're good," one of them said, "I promise to give you a beautiful present at the end of the week."

Layla dreamed of the present and no longer trembled; she

received a pretty missal with a holy image in the form of a bookmark. For many long years she tenderly leafed through it. The pages have yellowed, and the cover has faded. From time to time, Layla takes it out of her drawer and thinks of her childhood dreams ...

In vain she looked for faith, in between two clergies set against each other for centuries, or in the flame of a mystical tradition. She found only ashes.

Layla didn't have friends at the school. The days were as repetitious and monotonous as the boarders' uniforms.

At home Zebeida was bursting with joy: she was marrying her daughter to a truck driver. "Dressed like a gentleman, a true *khawaga*,[3] in his overalls. Five pounds a month, the handsome man." Zebeida filled the house with zaghareets: her hand on her mouth, her lips rounded, her tongue moving like a high speed metronome, she yelled forth her shrill cries, which then faded out with her breath, only to begin again with all her great joy.

On certain autumn days, the whole house was fragrant with the odor of rose or mint or orange flowers. In the bottom of a large still, Madam Morcos piled up flowers or their petals, brought from the countryside. She filled the channel around the container with water, set up a bottle below the faucet, heated the water, and then waited. Drop by drop, the essential oil of the rose, the mint, or the orange flowers, was condensed. Rose water was used to flavor all of the cakes and fruit salads. Mint and orange flowers healed stomach aches or abdominal pain.

Madam Morcos boasted that she made the best jams in the region. Her secret? Time and patience in order to cut the peels of innumerous bitter oranges into very fine slices and to watch over them as they cook. She also made mango, rose, and lemon syrups, and guava and carrot jellies. But her glory reached its height in her almond-stuffed dates and the juiciness of her stuffed grape leaves.

One episode which Layla had little taste for, and which she tried to avoid, was the preparation of the *samna*, the canned melted butter. For days and days a rancid odor clung to the house. The butter

---

[3] Khawaga: a foreign-style gentleman.

would arrive from the countryside in the form of large white sausages kneaded with salt—good butter for spreading. Alas! The operation consisted of boiling it down to samna by letting it simmer in a large pot for an entire day. The salt would separate from the butter, sink to the bottom and form a paste, the *morta*, intended for the crusts of the poor or the bread slices of rich connoisseurs. Madam Morcos put good samna, absolutely necessary for Egyptian cuisine, into square cans; for the whole year she stored the reserve of melted butter in cupboards where she dipped into it, ladleful by ladleful, according to need.

The doctor had died at the age of forty of angina pectoris. He had never done any exercise to compensate for the culinary talents of Madam Morcos, and to better digest all of the good samna that she lavished on him.

Each year after the harvest, the dwarf Khamis, whose name means Thursday, and Wahba the fool, accompanied the scribe—who came from the village to pay the Morcos family for the produce of their lands—to Cairo. The children loved these two clowns dearly.

Wahba had earlobes as disproportionately long as his body. He knew how to make them dance with a subtle movement of his jaw. Puffed up with pride, Khamis twirled his walking stick.

"Look at how well I dance," he said to Layla. "It's a tradition with the dwarves of our race. Are you laughing? The Pharaohs paid a lot to have dwarves perform sacred dances! Don't take on airs just because you go to school. It is written in the texts of the pyramids: 'The dead will dance like a dwarf before Osiris.' A man who comes to Kasr Hour for archeological digs told me so . . . You have to ask your mother to take you to Hour some day. I'll show you the digs, and the fields of sugar cane, wheat, and corn. And the house where your father was born. May God rest his soul!"

"Are you all dwarves in your family?"

"All of us! And so ugly that we make the *afreet* (demons) run away. Am I making you laugh? You'll see how well I know how to scare people."

And he grimaced so that his face was enlarged, and he seemed even stockier and smaller.

"In the past people were wise. They knew that the good God likes to laugh."

Wahba and the scribe gave Madam Morcos news of the cousins who had remained in the village, of the grandmother who had gone mad, and of her beautiful house which was falling into ruin.

The next day, after having slept at the house of the most senior uncle on the paternal side of the family, the dwarf, the fool and the scribe took the train again, a local one that, because it was cheaper, lingered in all the little stations. It was called *ashâsh*—the collector—because its cars and running boards disappeared under the crates of hens, the mountains of eggs and the sugar cane stalks, all carted along by a human anthill.

At the Morcos home, joy was in the air: Gamila was expecting a child.

"If you will allow it," said Zebeida to the grandmother," I'm going to take her to your house: her child will have your face, the beauty of the moon, your milky complexion, your rose-like cheeks."

And Gamila—all covered with jewels, veiled, made up, pretending timidity—came and sat at the grandmother's feet. Obviously pampered by her husband, she wouldn't stop talking about her happiness, in answer to the grandmother's questions, and Zebeida, joyfully talkative, was full of details: "Look," she said, "at the beautiful dress that he had made for her. Silk, madam, one pound per meter. What a generous man! And her shoes are just like a lady's ... Excuse me," she added hastily, when she saw Madam Morcos going by, "without any comparison to what you're wearing! And all of these bracelets! Her husband covers her with gold and pearls!"

"*Amma*," Gamila sometimes interrupted, "I want a mango."

"Go and find her one, quickly," said the grandmother to Zebeida. "The little one must not be born with the image of a mango on its skin!"

And Zebeida went to buy a mango on the other side of the one-eyed street lamp. When she didn't find any, she went around the whole neighborhood looking stunned, and then took the tramway all the way to the big market in Bab-Al-Louk. The grandmother always loosened her purse strings for such important things.

A tutor came to the house twice a week. This Mister Pahor had no title of glory other than that he was Coptic and the fact that he carried the name of Horus, the falcon, the sun god, the hero of legends. For centuries his ancestors had resisted the Islamic invasion and not converted. Did they pay the *djizzia*, the tax of the conquered? Did they take refuge in Upper Egypt like so many others? Mister Pahor never questioned the religion of his forefathers.

He was Coptic; proud and strong because he was a Copt. However, he had not succeeded in becoming a bursar, or a tax collector, or a mere ledger clerk, like the scribes of ancient times ... But he was a Copt. And, as if to prove it even more so—maybe to possible Abyssinian conquerors—he had a Coptic cross tattooed on the inside of each wrist.

He would have succeeded in filling up the suit he wore, if only he had been as well nourished as the person who had given it to him out of charity. But Mister Pahor was too poor; he ironed it, cleaned it, did his best to hide his skinny belly. He was almost a khawaga, a foreign man, with his white complexion, his long white hands. His mother, a good woman, took good care of him. Mister Pahor was just a little tutor, but he was a Copt.

He taught Arabic to Layla and her brother, and they liked to prolong the difficult Thursday and Sunday lessons by eating a good lunch with him. But Mister Pahor had to be begged to stay; one could see his nostrils flare, his mouth water, his eyes fill with delicious visions: the two opulent hens in a big pot, the molokheyah soup, made of that ancient succulent herb, grown between rows of cotton, simmered in chicken broth, seasoned with a mixture of roasted garlic and coriander. They begged Mister Pahor to taste it, to serve himself a lot with the rice cooked in broth and seasoned with thickened, creamy tomato sauce. And a few round slices of red onion. And for dessert, strawberries, or a good slice of chilled watermelon.

Mister Pahor had to be forced to stay for lunch!

He was cultured; he explained, for example, the meaning of

the word Copt: "Aegyptos: Het-ka-ptah," he said, as he slightly raised himself up on his elbows, "the-house-of-the-soul-of-Ptah," he translated as he puffed himself up enough to fill his suit. "Coptic means 'Egyptian.' When the Arabs occupied the country, they wrote our name in Arabic, and since there are no vowels in their writing, they wrote G-B-T, and that quickly became 'gypty': Copt."

"G-B-T," repeated Layla's brother, like a good student of the Jesuits. "I farted! Ha, ha, ha! I farted!"[4]

The kids were doubled up with laughter, but Mister Pahor, who didn't know French, continued his explanation unperturbed. He was proud of his ancestors and he took pleasure in a climate of persecution.

However, one day fortune smiled timidly at him. In spite of the advice of Madam Morcos, he married the daughter of a rich peasant. She had a heart condition. To entice him to marry her, the father gave a building with the furniture for a large apartment. She didn't tolerate married life well and only left her bed to go to her tomb. Half of her property went to Mister Pahor, who hurriedly arranged a new marriage and had many children, all Copts, all a bit contemptuous of the rest of humankind.

The Copt stands out because of his attachment to the Egyptian earth that hid him during times of persecution. He is surrounded by countless numbers of mummies who strangely resemble him. When he dies, a hole is dug for him in the soil in which is mixed, in unknown proportions, the dust of mummies …

In the countryside around Rodah, one can see a thousand-year-old sight: the *saquiah*. A gamoussah—a female buffalo—is harnessed to a horizontal wheel attached to a large wheel carrying earthenware jugs. The beast goes around, the jugs draw water, lift it up and pour it into the channels that crisscross the fields. The eyes of the gamoussah are blindfolded. She musn't stop, the dizziness would stop her dead in her tracks; she doesn't know that she is turning round and round.

Layla watches the saquiah nostalgically. What efforts were deployed by her teachers to weave a blindfold across her own eyes!

[4] The pun is based on the sound of the letters, G, B, and T. If said aloud one after the other, they sound like "J'ai pété," which means "I farted."

While sewing or embroidering in the company of her mother and aunts, the principles of a code of honor had been instilled in her without her realizing it: a Copt who marries a Moslem rejects the faith of her ancestors and dishonors herself. The woman who marries a non-Coptic Christian demeans herself just as much in the eyes of the community. Marrying a Catholic Copt is hardly better: how can one trust people who rallied to a foreign pope? Such a marriage cannot be tolerated except under one express condition: that it be celebrated in the orthodox Coptic church in such a way as to bring the heretic back to the fold. In any marital union, the man or woman who converts to the other's religion is dishonored.

What she learned much later is that the Moslem majority bitterly reproached the Copts for their strange obstinacy in calling attention to themselves; and the Moslems were even more irritated, because to them, the religion of the Prophet was much more rational, in their eyes, than that of the Christians, which was filled with a sort of witchcraft, with that God who is a Trinity and that bread that transforms into flesh, the wine that transforms into blood, that way of devouring Christ whole in each crumb of bread, in each drop of blood: sorcery or cannibalism.

Must Layla continue to turn in the circle designated for her? In order to irrigate what? Layla remained Coptic, but she married Hussein, a Moslem, one of those "traitors," one of those fragile reeds whose ancestors were not strong enough to keep the religion of their ancestors. She asks herself:

"Hussein's ancestors first worshipped the Egyptian gods, then they converted to the Christian god, and finally they worshipped Allah! My family continued to travel the same circle after the coming of Allah into Egypt. I married Hussein; they cried out in indignation; then they forgot. Hussein is dead. Another circle needs to be drawn. Perhaps a spiral ..."

The private school tuition weighed heavily on the budget of the little family. The doctor was dead, and he had left two buildings under construction and much disorder in the accounts. The Rodah house had brought some comfort but little income. Divided up, a

ny intuition. I get it from my father."

Henceforth, it was she who gave advice. Thanks to the Bank of gypt, industries multiplied, in Mehallah-el-Kobrah, in Beida ... The cloth was beautiful and well made; it sold well. Egypt revived a glorious tradition as ancient as its mummies. Her personal savings exhausted, Madam Morcos drew brand new *talaris*[5] and shillings from the children's money boxes. The capital doubled, the double of the capital doubled ...

Undoubtedly Madam Morcos really did get it from her father. And her brothers and sisters, too. They liked order, knew how to create it from disorder and how to be resourceful in the face of a storm. A family stronghold made of caution, scrupulous honesty, proud moral standards: Puritanism and superiority.

Those uncles and aunts who possessed that strange and solid knowledge of human ugliness, and camouflaged it underneath the beautiful image they made of themselves, have disappeared. Layla learned from them to take the family name seriously, a name transmitted by the men and protected by the women. On their death beds, their faces curiously resembled the mummies preserved in the museums, preserved in an unusual truth, stripped of life, reconnected to past millennia.

It is a weighty heritage to carry, which Layla cherishes but doesn't know what to do with.

When the Second World War exploded, Layla was still a very little school girl.

That year, Madam Morcos had decided that her daughter would learn English ... and hired a German governess. The latter arrived at the end of June when the last days of school were dragging on, with their heavy gusts of hot air, and there was nostalgia for the ocean waves.

The horrible word "governess!" What is more, Frederika was heavy and stocky, and Layla's friends took her for her mother. Layla couldn't stand it, and she promised herself not to suffer the foreign woman's presence for long.

[5] Talari: there are five talaris in a pound and four shillings in a talari.

On the day of the distribution of school prizes, they left for Alexandria, while the uncles, aunts and cousins sailed for Europe. They set up on the second floor of a yellow house overlooking the Sidi Bishr beach. After the declaration of war, they were very worried about those who had taken the sea route. From up on the yellow veranda, they anxiously watched for the boats.

As soon as the early morning began, Layla crossed the coastal road that separated her from the beach, and swam and rolled in the sand under the sun. All around her, beach umbrellas sprouted like mushrooms. She couldn't care less about them, didn't look for the protection offered by their shade. Her only desire was to lose herself in the water, the sand and the sun.

Her brothers were good swimmers. They dared to dive into the devil's hole where the waves and water currents smashed into each other in a muffled din. They were afraid of nothing, and came home late in the evening to prove it.

In the evening, Layla took a walk with Zebeida, which supremely displeased Frederika: to prefer the company of a servant over hers! But the governess couldn't savor the joys of the street, nor recognize the familiar characters of the corniche, similar to those from the banks of the Nile. Every afternoon during nap time, Layla set herself to constructing the plan of smothering Frederika underneath a pile of cushions!

After three days of a trying voyage, the uncles, aunts and cousins returned, piled like sardines, on the last boat. Three days of nausea to acquire the right to read in the newspapers—at breakfast, in the evening, at whiskey hour—about the battles and miseries of other people. At the Rotary Club and the Gezireh Sporting Club, the strategies were numerous, some betting on the German forces, others on the Allies' ability to resist.

The rumors about the persecution of the Jews were already spreading, with millions of good people witnessing the sight and saying nothing. Layla's little world was shaken, without suspecting that the Arab world would one day pay for the crimes of the Nazis.

As soon as classes began again, Frederika perceived that she was not welcome. She left.

The comfortable and peaceful life of the Morcos family continued. However, death was always playing with life. One day, Zebeida
arrived with the tale of her daughter's misfortunes; she had just
brought a stillborn into the world.

"Nine months of waiting and pain for nothing!" she moaned.
"My daughter has a Karina watching her so she can give her the evil
eye."

"A Karina, what's that?" Layla inquired.

"It's a sister … a double that one doesn't see. I saw her in my
dream. She was waist-high; I touched her head. A soft and mean
head!"

"And what did you do, Zebeida?" asked the grandmother.

"When I saw the dead child, I sent Ibrahim to buy a jug, a *rotoli*
of salt and bread. I asked the midwife to give me the placenta, and
I placed it in the jug with the salt and bread. Then I dug a hole at the
threshold of the house and I buried the jug … The spirit of the placenta will become a new child for my daughter."

"May God hear you!" said the grandmother.

But Gamila's misfortunes were not over. The spirit of the placenta never became another child. Zebeida resorted to all sorts of
charms in order to prevent further miscarriages … She had her
daughter do the tour of the saints' tombs, Copt or Moslem. She had
her roll on the ground around these burial places, in the hope of
capturing a soul seeking reincarnation.

Her wailing resembled incantations:

"I'll call him Shahät (beggar), providing he lives! Who can be
envious of a beggar and give him the evil eye?"

"May he live, and I'll call him Zabbal (garbage man)! Who can
be envious of a garbage man?"

"I'll call him Mallim: one thousandth of a pound, that's nothing at all!"

"And what if it were a girl, Zebeida?"

Zebeida suddenly stopped her lamenting and, stupefied, looked
at Layla.

"A girl? But everything would have to be started over! In order
to keep her husband, Gamila has to have a child who is worth some-

thing. So what do they teach you at school?"

But nothing worked, and Gamila's spouse lost patience. At the end of four years of waiting, he said to her three times: "You are repudiated," and Gamila moved to the Morcos home. She waited for her husband or God to take pity on her. She prayed five times a day.

And her husband, Osta Sayed, came back for her one day. There were never-ending discussions, big gestures with their arms and hands: Osta Sayed had said three times: "You are repudiated." For him to take back his wife, he needed a *mohallel*, a man who would accept to marry Gamila for a day and then to repudiate her. Enough time to make love and undo the divorce!

In return for five Egyptian pounds, they found a mohallel. The man "tasted" Gamila's "little honey," and, jealous, Osta Sayed bitterly regretted what he'd done.

"Oh, the bitch! She's taking revenge on me! I'm suffering, and she's enjoying herself. Oh, the bitch!"

But Gamila loved her handsome truck driver, with his glorious moustache and his fat belly. The experience with the mohallel was just one more trial added to her sterility. The only thing was that Osta Sayed couldn't understand that.

Everything went well, because Gamila was poor, and the spouse of one night had no interest in refusing her a divorce.

"God's ways," said the grandmother, "are hidden from man. May he protect Gamila and bring her happiness. She's a fine girl."

Until seventh grade, Layla was an excellent student; the nuns passed her directly into fifth grade.[6] That's when she began to neglect her homework and become undisciplined.

At her uncle's house she discovered her grandfather's marvelous library, and she took from it indiscriminately, steeping herself in tears, laughter and mystery.

With her year in sixth grade, she had missed the study of Greek mythology. As for Egyptian mythology, the young colonized girls were supposed to be completely unaware of it! Thanks to the library,

[6] In the old French system, the counting of grades began with the eleventh and went to the first.

Layla filled in that gap. She discovered the myth of Isis, which blends poetry with death and love … the legend of Seth and Osiris, next to which the story of Cain and Abel seems quite dull.

Osiris, the older one, reigned over Egypt, civilized its inhabitants, taught them to cultivate the earth, grind wheat, press grapes. He instituted laws so that men would live in peace. Seth, the younger brother, gathered all of the evil on earth and killed his brother, the good king Osiris …

Death, which plays with life like black sails under the sun, carried away Layla's grandmother: Teta died at the hour when the shades are closed to prevent the light from coming in.

Layla watched Madam Morcos bathe the body, adorn it with the entire funeral trousseau that the grandmother had prepared for herself, and envelop it in her white bridal bedspread.

Zebeida arrived with two women, their veils blowing in the wind, stumbling with pain. In insane agitation, they slapped their faces, pretended to rip their clothing, and to tear at their breasts. For a brief moment, Layla recalled the superb pantomime of the hired women mourners on Ramses' tomb.

"Good people, help me!" cried out Zebeida, "our *baraka*[7] has disappeared. A great woman full of grace. Good people, help me!"

Black forms—female relatives and friends—invaded the house, in tears or with an inquisitive expression. For three long days, they ate in honor of the dead woman's soul. And on the third day, the priest blessed the food, the house and the black shapes. He liberated the premises from the soul of the grandmother and the latter from the places she had been attached to. A blessing, water, a branch of greenery, a flame.

The black shadows returned on the seventh day, the fifteenth, and the fortieth, after the death.

The Morcoses had large banquets to prepare and little time to suffer. Layla, excluded from the living room, bustled about with the women cooks.

Madam Morcos, who was conscious of belonging to the urban elite which refused to make a spectacle of itself by excessive wail-

[7] Baraka: luck, fortune.

ing, spoke with disdain of the customs of Upper Egypt:

"Imagine that they don't even sweep! And they wait for the meals to arrive all prepared from the neighboring houses ..."

The grandmother was going to rest in an abandoned dwelling in a large cemetery, along the edge of the desert, in a red mountain, in the shadow of royal poincianas and eucalyptus trees.

The morticians had put her in her coffin the day after her death. They had set the cover of the coffin in place with large screws bearing Coptic crosses.

What does all this pomp serve other than to protect the deceased from the Earth God, from Gheb, with his hairy body, husband of the Sky Goddess, Nout, who everyday swallows a sun and each morning gives birth to a new one?

The morticians had placed the coffin on a lower ground floor shelf, near to that of the grandfather.

The grandmother's marvelous smile, the grandfather's severe look ... It was once again a new marriage.

The beaming grandmother's face still lived in Layla's heart, like a soft presence, warm and luminous. Layla began to love death, as she loved the desert, to love the world of the dead, which was as old as ancient Egypt. "Everything that is the most beautiful in this country," she thought, "has its origin in a tomb."

Spring is celebrated every year. Everything is reborn from the earth, people breathe in the fresh breeze: Cham-al-Nissim!

New life? Layla is waiting for it to burst forth from anywhere. From a black hole, from death or despair ...

She is waiting.

CHAPTER 3
Secret Doors

In ancient Arab houses, there was always a secret door: *bab sirr*. It has disappeared in European-style houses, but love remains a secret threatened by scandal. In rural Egypt, everything is done to protect the honor of girls: the child is constantly under surveillance, a charm bracelet—the *kholkhal*, the sound of which indicates her presence at each step she takes—is put on her ankle; to give her a defense against love, her clitoris is excised; she is constantly lectured about her honor. But she discovers her secret door. The tall stalks of corn and sugar cane protect her loves. And the man—in order to give her pleasure, in spite of her excision, in order to win time or dream that he is winning it, to impart a magical refinement to the senses and give back to the woman the passion stolen from her by surgery—the man takes hashish. And when he can no longer make love, he takes some more so he can dream he is giving her pleasure.

Taboos and secret doors increase in number. In order to feed guilt? To prohibit innocence?

A collective code protects tradition, the excision of girls, hashish. Hashish! Fifteen years of prison for whomever is caught smoking it. But the notable offers some to the doctor paying a visit. A sort of brown stone, soft as compressed cork, is casually given to the newly married man—to be made into a ring, no doubt! Everyone knows where the hideout—the *ghorza* of the hashish smokers, the *haschaschin*—is located. Everyone knows that hashish makes you very hungry, and that Middle Eastern pastry shops selling cakes kneaded with butter, cream, sugar and honey, are open until dawn, to calm this hunger. Love is forbidden, but everyone laughs when words stagger and take the form of sensual poses.

At fifteen years of age, Layla already knows how to recognize eroticism in the words and gazes of boys. They go out in masses into the streets of Cairo in order to escape being smothered by a life that passes by next to love. They walk, hand in hand, their eyes greedy, their throats dry, at the sight of girls who also walk hand in hand, and who quietly laugh and pretend not to hear the "dishonest propositions," discreetly whispered. The boys finish their evening at the movies in front of a love film, and they hurl insults at love. If they have any money left over, they go to prostitutes, and then spit on the prostitutes.

When she was fifteen, Layla attended the marriage of a Bedouin.

It was in Agami on a summer's eve. Friends had invited her for a few days to their magnificent house overlooking a beach of white sand at the edge of a turquoise sea. Their *boab* (doorman), Abd'Allah, was getting married. He was rich. To bring his fiancée with her trousseau, he had sent for her, not with carts pulled by exhausted donkeys, but with large Ford trucks. The chairs, chests of drawers, and kitchen utensils had been unloaded, as had the pink, blue and pistachio green eiderdowns which seemed to say: "Look carefully at us, this evening we will see love."

The fiancée appeared, adorned and made up like a sugar doll for the birthday of the Prophet. Terrified. The drums were beating, the reed pipes were singing, the women were trying to outdo each other in zaghareets. With the groom, the men made a circle around one of them who was dancing as he twirled his cane.

The women surrounded the sugar doll. Two among them felt particularly proud: the *dallalah*, who had negotiated the dowry, and the *ballamah*, who had bathed and powdered the bride and removed all the hair from her body with caramel wax.

The celebration was at its height when Abd'Allah withdrew for an instant with his fiancée and returned satisfied. The ballanah and the dallalah showered the bride with attention and returned to show the audience a handkerchief all covered with blood. She was a virgin:

..e celebration could continue.

Abd'Allah feasted for two days. The doll remained stiff, surrounded by all the women drinking, eating and crying out like birds
of prey. A scandal was brewing, however, which Layla discovered in
snatches of allusions and whispers: the fiancée was not a virgin, she
loved a boy her own age. Her marriage had been decided upon by her
father, a rich camel owner who preferred Abd'Allah, already a father
and grandfather, but rich! The blood on the handkerchief came from
a chicken gullet; cleverly positioned, it had simulated virginity ...

Layla was sixteen when one of her classmates, a girl from an
important family, left the boarding school to marry. One month later,
it was learned that her husband had been killed by the king's soldiers.
She was beautiful, she was rich. To cover up the scandal, she was
quickly remarried to one of her cousins. Everyone knew, in fact, that
her first marriage had taken place by order of the king; that her husband had left on a mission by order of the king; and that the king was
visiting the young bride. His honor wounded, the husband had tried
to return. And the soldiers had killed him.

Besides, Layla was told, the king respected virginity. When he
wanted a girl, he got her married before coming to visit her. It was as
difficult for the girls of an important family to resist him, as it was for
a peasant girl to refuse the village notables.

Layla thus learned that virginity was her most precious possession, marriage her destiny, and love, her ruin.

In spite of secret doors, sensuality, and the scandals buzzing
round about, she was taught modesty.

Her brothers and cousins had every right; Layla had none, and
she didn't complain about it. But this universal indulgence toward
men's sensuality, this insulting right they had to feel spiteful toward
young women who followed their own desires—all of this revolted
her. A tragedy for the women, a huge laugh for the men.

Her muted revolt transformed into a feeling of disgust for sensuality.

CHAPTER 4

Under the Red Flag

One year after the death of her mother, Madam Morcos put a white collar on her black dress and began a new life. Through her sisters-in-law, who had considerable social status thanks to their husbands' jobs, she re-established contact with her friends of old. The social events at which she could be present—funerals, condolence visits, and charity balls—were abundant. Madam Morcos did not in any way take advantage of the condolence visits. She went by choice, in the strictest privacy, to show a discreet sympathy.

On the other hand, she imposed no moderation on herself when it came to the work of charitable organizations: preparing bandages for the Red Crescent, founding a school to teach poor girls the art of service. To help subsidize these activities, she and her sisters-in-law and their friends organized celebrations, raffles, garden parties, and large dinners.

Other feminine activities filled Madam Morcos with admiration. She envied the teams of young women fighting malaria in Upper Egypt, and the Daughters of the Nile, united around Doreya Chafik, to work for the liberation of women. She would like to have been Hoda Cha'raoui, the "mother" of all Egyptians, who participated in Wafd's independence movement, or else Seza Nabaraoui, the former chief editor of *The Egyptian Woman*, a journal published in French, meant for foreign women and rich women, that advocated the imitation of admirable French morals, but also the renewal of Egyptian national pride.

Madam Morcos sympathized with all women who opposed the *Ulemas'* (Koranic scholars) decrees, and who demanded reforms and tirelessly endeavored to protect women from polygamy, divorce and the omnipotence of fathers and husbands. But she had learned from her father that it was considered impolite for a woman to make herself noticed. She liked to think of herself as a woman conscious of her value, but not as a suffragette.

A new life was also beginning for Layla, who was quietly growing wiser.

She had a lot of cousins, libertines who claimed to respect nothing, and prudes who blushed and didn't dare get near her. Some of them spoke French, others English, and all spoke Arabic.

Since she was well brought up, Layla always acted as if she wasn't interested in her brothers' and cousins' friends. When one of them would look at her insistently, and he was a nice-looking man, she would, however, prolong that look in her dreams. But to her girlfriends she would say: "He's too stupid!"

Her favorite cousins pulled her hair. She would bite or scratch them. They exchanged books or ideas. They learned to dance together. But social constraints weighed crushingly on both lawful enterprises and hidden intrigues.

The streets and dance halls were full of European soldiers. The girls who went out with them wore puffed-up hairdos, soldiers' epaulettes, and short skirts. They stirred up murmurs of surprise, scandal, fear and envy. The women in black were shocked by them.

"Happiness does not lie at the end of that path," they said. "They're losing their reputation there ... The flashy uniform camouflages all sorts of family backgrounds. There're so many risks to marrying beneath one's station!"

"A life of vice," added the good young people from their provinces. "We lock up the girls in our families and protect them from the devil. Oh! Those city people!"

Layla remembers the day she'd met Hussein. It was in March 1946, a day of Khamsin. The desert wind was blowing at more than one hundred kilometers per hour, suspending myriads of wildly moving grains of sand in a sky that had turned yellow, then orange-colored, then red. Trees were uprooted, small boats capsized in the Nile. Shortly afterwards, in Beirut, there was a "rain of blood."

Layla was in the street in Garden City. She was quietly returning home when she was attacked by grains of sand that hacked her face as they swept into her nose, her eyes and her ears.

She took refuge at her cousin Hanna's, who lived with his parents on the top floor of a sumptuous apartment building on the banks of the Nile. On cold winter days, from his office and the terrace, they marveled at the sun's play of light on the buildings and the Nile, with its slowly moving feluccas. Far off were the pyramids of Gizeh, like drops of light; even farther away was the step pyramid of Sakkarah, then the mysterious desert. That day, they could barely make out the sun through an immense reddish brown glow. The Khamsin had covered Layla with a ghostly veil.

"In the name of Allah, the Compassionate, the Merciful!" said Hanna as he opened the door.

"In the name of the living Christ," replied Layla.

Their laughter burst forth and the aunt rushed up to see what was happening. Layla the refugee spent lovely hours with Hanna and his friend Hussein; "comrade Hanna, comrade Hussein," as they called each other. They spoke of Marx, of Trotsky and of Rosa Luxembourg.

"All Jews," said Layla.

"No, Miss Scholar," retorted Hussein, "citizens of the world."

They spoke of their readings: Gide, Nietzsche by way of Gide, and Sartre, Simone de Beauvoir, Albert Camus.

When Layla returned home a few hours late, her mother bombarded her with questions.

"Hussein Zaghloul? That name means something to me. Isn't he the son of my friend Fatma? What's he like?"

"He resembles," said Layla, "the cut-off head of Amenemhat II."

"What?" said Madam Morcos, alarmed.

"The head of a sphinx."

And she described his slightly bulging eyes concealed by eyelids that never entirely opened, his lion-like ears in the shape of a canopy, his large jaw, his prominent cheekbones, the bags beneath his eyes ... But also the very frizzy crew cut and his big laugh.

"Your Amenemhat is not handsome!"

"No, but his statues are beautiful, and Hussein is very funny. I bet he dances very well, he's so slender and tall."

"What a pity," Madam Morcos said dreamily. "His mother was very beautiful. She took after a Circassian grandmother. We used to hold social gatherings in our fathers' houses and we were great friends ... Those were the good old days."

"Do you miss them?"

"No. Life separates friends. Fatma married a modest professor of Arabic. It's said he spent time in prison because he was a Communist ... I never saw her again."

The Morcoses had a cabin in Stanley used by many cousins as a changing room when they were on vacation in Alexandria. It was there that Madam Morcos and Madam Zaghloul met again.

While Layla and Hussein swam, dove, sped out onto the open sea in light canoes and returned astride large waves, the two women recounted their lives to each other.

The crowd abandoned the beach. Solitude spread around the cabins, and under the star-studded sky, Madam Morcos and Madam Zaghloul continued to reel off all of their memories until the watchman chased them away.

On a vocabulary board, Hussein, Hanna and Layla lined up Arabic letters.

"Forget tradition," said Hussein. "Each person will pronounce the letters as he sees fit. The accents on the consonants and the punctuation were only invented to help out conquered foreigners. Among them, the Egyptians ... You have to learn to read Arabic with a lot of liberty; that way people will maybe stop dogmatizing about revealed texts."

"You'd have yourself burned for a heretic," said Layla.

"Too bad! My father did prison time before me ..."

Hussein seduces his world. Wise little Layla, who always needs punctuated texts, learns audacity. Hussein makes her see the misery surrounding their comfort: the cook who spends all morning long near the hell of the fire in order to prepare the meal; the *soufragui* who has to run on the sand in order to serve them their meals hot. And farther away, the landless peasant, the old man without a home; overpopulation already, bodies piled into rooms built of raw earth before being heaped into tombs, children's eyes abandoned to the flies...

Pushed by his father, who had suffered the frustrations of the intellectual, Hussein had studied agriculture. He wanted to diversify the crops and change the methods of husbandry in order to decolonize the Egyptian earth. A property owner, he had taken back a part of his land from the family of farmers who cultivated it: five feddans, or two hectares, a modest beginning. He had planted castor oil plants, which were in shortage because of the war; with the enthusiasm of a pioneer, he had reintroduced an ancient crop into earth that never ceased repeating itself: clover, cotton, wheat, clover, cotton, wheat. Never-ending servitude.

The harvest was good ... But the peasants, deprived of their work as day laborers, driven to the brink of despair, began planning their revenge: to enter Hussein's house one evening to kill him. A servant who refused to be bribed warned his master. Hussein had the peasants come and he promised them a portion of the profits. But when the end of the war came, castor oil was imported at a better price, and there were no profits. Profoundly marked by this event, Hussein once again rented his land to the peasants and henceforth lived schizophrenically: as both a Communist and a landowner.

"While we're here," he repeated, "settled comfortably by the seashore, the fellah toils in order not to die. When we think it's best, we go to the village and we throw him out because we're the owners. Do you expect that to go on forever? The peasant will rise up and massacre us."

However, there was hope on the morrow of Hitler's defeat. Good and brave intellectuals were attempting to change the world. There was already talk of the great dam of Assouan, which would permit the cultivation of 500,000 hectares of desert land. They were going to build it, but when and at what price? The demographic explosion was going to devour everything, like a monster with a thousand mouths, and leave an entire nation gasping for breath.

Hussein had inherited forty feddans from his father, which he then rented to innumerable peasants: maybe eighty families who themselves employed day laborers. A bursar kept a tight rein on the accounts.

As for himself, he planned to begin his studies again and hesitated between a career as an engineer and a career as an economist. Trinity College in Cambridge? The University of Paris? He finally chose Paris, law, and economics.

Layla had just passed her baccalaureate with honors. Some of her classmates were already united with brilliant matches: a diplomat, a doctor, an employee of the Canal Company ...

"Arranged marriages are the best," said right-thinking people. "Love? All that requires is a spanking."

Layla had neither a father nor a fortune. Nor even beauty that could save the situation. No one crowded around to ask her hand in marriage. However, one day one of her paternal aunts made a timid attempt:

"Your daughter has cousins," she said to Madam Morcos. "Let her choose one. I'll see to it that he marries her."

Since Madam Morcos had not responded to her initiatives, it was the aunt herself who made the choice: a cousin with romantic eyes. She tried to negotiate the marriage. Layla felt transformed into an acre of land. The cousin's mother said:

"I'll give her my solitaire and I'll furnish her house. My son will inherit one hundred feddans from his father and as much from me. In the meantime, I'll transfer my house in Zamalek into his name."

"I'll talk about it with my daughter," said Madam Morcos.

"You'll make her hear the voice of reason ..."

Very fortunately, Madam Morcos didn't really want her daughter to marry: from her own marriage she had kept that bitter taste of ashes ...

Thus it was in the joy of a summer without the threat of mar-

riage that Fakhr-el-Nissa made her entry into Layla's life. She was
Hussein's sister, and her name meant "the glory of women."

A small head, a replica of Tutankhamen's, burst forth out of
the collar of her striped percale blouse like a lotus. She had a splen-
did head of flowing brown hair, pulled back into a thick braid that
fell all the way to her waist, and a pretty, tender, malicious and intelligent smile.

Slim, sure of herself, full of spirit and an ardor for life, Fakhr-
el-Nissa felt at ease in her body as if she were in a sacred vase.

Layla had been taught that eroticism and a concern for one's
body meant vice and sin. Fakhr-el-Nissa had been told just the opposite: that it was necessary to use them with one's husband—against
one's husband!—in order to keep hold of him or to hold him back.
And she had cared for her body with taste and joy.

She returned from Paris for a short vacation, bringing back
with her the life of a world believed to have been buried under
rubble. Paris was still the City of Light; you could live there and
study there as always!

She recounted: the Sorbonne, the Institute of Political Science...,
the barges on the Seine. Madam Morcos listened, her eyes shining. And
Layla passionately observed her mother's expression.

Was it thus possible? Paris!

Fakhr-el-Nissa left again. That same day, a bearded Sikh passed
by in an imposing white turban. He scrutinized Layla's face, studied
the lines on her hand and predicted an excellent marriage for her,
though belated, years of study and great success.

Who hasn't had his Sikh or gypsy to give him the crazy hope of
making something of his life?

Fakhr-el-Nissa had also had her Sikh, but it was the great Seza
Nabaroui who had demonstrated to her, texts in hand, that in fact
Islam gave as many rights to women as the most advanced legislation.
All one had to do for proof was to consult theologians like El-Afghani
or the Sheikh Mohamed Abdou, who do a modern and feminist reading of the Koran. From that moment on, her future was all laid out:
she would be an example to the women of Egypt, would incite them
to fully utilize the rights accorded to them by Islam.

Fakhr-el-Nissa had decided to make her career elsewhere, other than in marriage.

A foreign wind blew through all of society. Everyone left for a few years or a few months in order to perfect the training they had received in Egypt. Yahia, already an engineer, who had joined the army and was lining up stars on his epaulettes, didn't have the time to think of other horizons. But her youngest brother, his cousins— with Bachelor's degrees in letters, law or science—all of them were preparing to leave so they could put the finishing touches on their careers ... and also maybe to look for a life of temporary debauchery far from the malevolent eyes of puritanical families.

They had nothing to worry about: they were males and landowners, and moreover, the work of their fellahins dispensed them from having to work anytime soon.

Meanwhile in Upper Egypt, the peasants, their wives and their children were fighting the cotton worms or harvesting its flowers.

As for Layla, she continued to live on water, sun, sand and wind. Everything would be more delicate for her. Her uncle, who didn't dare risk speaking with her about her honor and her virginity, said:

"Paris is too cold for you. Pursue your studies here like Kawthar. We have very good universities."

So Layla went with Kawthar to Arabic literature classes. Referring to books overloaded with notes, the professors dogmatically explained the meaning of the texts ... She preferred Hussein's boldness.

She enjoyed herself, however, in Kawthar's circle of friends. She participated in group outings to public parks and Port Fouad.

Kawthar got engaged. Ram's blood flowed freely the day the contract was signed, after which the two young people had many years of schooling ahead of them before they could consummate their marriage. They were allowed to see each other and go out together in the company of friends. Thus were they protected against the devil's temptations.

So Layla made the decision to leave, to uproot herself, to live more intensely, perhaps to the detriment of happiness.

She used all the ammunition of a girl of seventeen. First tears, all day and all night long. She did as a child would: she evaluated the look in her mother's face to determine what would be possible to get from her, then she used her will to wrench it out of her.

It was the year of revolt and repression: university and factory strikes disrupted all activity. From their barracks, situated where the Nile Hilton Hotel is today, English troops fired with their machine guns, the 21st of February, into the masses of demonstrators. That year the National Committee of Workers and Students came into existence and was then dismantled. Hussein was a member; he also carried a Communist Party card. During his vacation in Alexandria, his house in Cairo had been searched from top to bottom. Fortunately, Fakhr-el-Nissa was warned in time, and she had managed to make all of the compromising papers and books disappear.

Layla suspected nothing. Hussein spoke of his fear of the peasants and left to resume his studies in Paris. But in reality he was afraid of being arrested.

In the darkened house, Layla pursued her strategy based on tears. Until the day when all of Madam Morcos's advisers agreed: "So let her leave!"

Madam Morcos, her heart full of fear, looked at Layla. Her aunts showered her with advice. Then they bustled about to prepare for her departure. They ran all over the department stores in order to buy her an outfit. They plied their needles at double speed to alter her ready-to-wear clothes.

One winter morning, Layla arrived in Paris on the train from Marseilles. Fakhr-el-Nissa was waiting for her at the station.

Quite naturally, their first words were in French. And then Layla heard a little voice within her saying: "You're Egyptian, and you speak French; these French, they only speak their own language."

"Fakhr-el-Nissa," she said hesitatingly, "let's speak Arabic, please!"

Thus was her nationalism timidly born.

When Fakhr-el-Nissa set her up in a pretty little hotel in Saint-Germain-des-Prés, Layla felt afraid for her honor and her virginity. Was her neighbor on the landing going to force open her door? She spent her first evening on the lookout. All of the hotel noises seemed dubious to her. Her anguish seemed intolerable. Toward midnight she was tempted to get it over with, to go knock on her neighbor's door, to get rid of her honor and her virginity ...

She awoke just as she had fallen asleep.

Layla went to visit the nuns of the Mother of God; in the dark hallways of their building, she met a few friends and a good number of former school mistresses. They tried fervently to turn her away from her project of going to the Sorbonne, a den of iniquity. They suggested the Catholic Institute; it was then that she remembered that she was Coptic, orthodox, heretical, and promised to the eternal flames of hell. Vice for vice, flame for flame, she preferred the Sorbonne and didn't return to the nuns.

Shortly afterward, she caught Fakhr-el-Nissa in the act of kissing a boy right on the mouth, smack in the middle of the library, seeming to defy the entire world. Layla was shocked and thought: "She is a lost girl. Paris is a den of iniquity. My uncle was absolutely right!" She said nothing about it to anyone, kept her indignation to herself, and then forgot all about it.

At every street corner, it seemed, young people, adults, and old people were kissing each other. On the quays of the metro, the banks of the Seine, the bridges of Paris, in the countryside. Layla even saw black boys kissing blond girls, and black girls kissing blond boys!

That brought back a memory—that of the day when, with Zebeida in the streetcar, they had seen a whole family of Blacks sitting across from them: the mother, the son, two daughters. All of them were well dressed in Western-style short dresses, suit and tie. What a shock! Not that they felt any prejudice: the doormen, the soufraguis of their family homes were Blacks, faithful servants, fine people, with a savory language that, without any ulterior motive, they had fun imitating. They liked them a lot, those Nubians, Sudanese, ethnically white, furthermore, whose skin color made the whiteness of their turbans stand out. Quite simply, they weren't used to seeing them rich and dressed like Westerners.

By the spring, Layla had already changed quite a bit. She wanted to live the songs that spoke of love and which she had been humming for years. She imagined, passionately, a first ideal kiss, unreal, which would stop the movement of the earth.

But each time the occasion seemed to arise, she would shrink back into her shell of the well-brought-up girl, behind a sort of silly laugh.

Would Hussein dare to? Will he dare?

She runs into him under the chestnut trees in the Luxembourg Gardens. He invites her to have coffee with him at Capoulade's, tells her about his projects, his readings, tells her what she should think and believe. She is fascinated.

But he doesn't dare to kiss her. And she doesn't dare let him understand that he can dare: she remains imprisoned in her respectability, painfully controlling her gestures. With foreign women Hussein is bold; but with an Egyptian woman, moreover a Copt, the daughter of a friend of his mother's, his best friend's cousin, he keeps a respectful distance.

Hussein stays late to talk, with his crew cut and his big comforting laugh. They leave each other with much tenderness and the memory of the ocean waves and the sandstorm.

Layla is assiduous in her philosophy course.

Madam Morcos covered the furniture, the chandeliers, the paintings, even the portrait of her husband, framed in black, and that of her father, embroidered with flowers, with unbleached linen dust covers. With the help of Zebeida and the household servants, she removed the dust from the Persian carpets by beating them with the lids of cooking pots, then wrapped the carpets in newspaper, rolled them up and stored them in a room on the terrace, with moth balls.

She double-locked the house. Equipped with her set of keys and innumerable suitcases, she took the train to Alexandria, the boat to Marseilles, and then again the train to Paris. Henceforth, there was nothing more urgent for her than to watch over the honor of her daughter by not leaving her alone in Paris.

The Rodah house would wait in the dark under dust covers, dust and spider webs. As for Zebeida, she had found herself without a roof over her head, armed with the little money that Madam Morcos had given her and the bundle of things with which she had arrived ten years earlier.

Madam Zaghloul, who was richer, kept her servants. She also left. The crossing was joyful, the stay in Paris even more so. The two old friends met again as in old times, they laughed about nothing, just for the pleasure; at age fifty they discovered in themselves new beauty; they ran around to the theaters, the cinema, the museums, and didn't leave out the tea rooms and couture houses. Had they erased fifteen years of widowhood?

Shortly after her arrival in Paris, Madam Zaghloul discovered, on the fifth floor of a beautiful apartment building, an apartment that was sunnier than Madam Morcos's on the ground floor. It had two tiny balconies that reminded one of the verandas of Cairo, with a view of the Seine and the Statue of Liberty. Another advantage of this apartment was that it could be divided into three, such that Hussein, Fakhr-el-Nissa and their mother each had their own private room.

Between a visit to a museum and the rounds of the department stores, the two women, who had transported with them, in their huge suitcases, all of the ingredients necessary for cooking delectable Egyptian dishes, treated their children, more than once, to elegant dinners.

During the course of these dinners, they debated many ideas:

"Every good Moslem," said Fakhr-el-Nissa, "must pay alms to the poor before praying and making the pilgrimage to Mecca!"

"Do you know," commented Hussein, "that after death, two angels armed with whips will ask you questions about Islam? Be careful if you answer incorrectly! We'd do well to practice a bit. God's word, for example ..."

"... It comes from man's heart in order to express God's desire. The different revelations are the expressions of this same desire."

"First whipping! Let's go on … Holy war, the jihad?"

"The Crusades falsified everything. Islam is the religion of tolerance. The Prophet's intention is ecumenical. He is looking for a common ground with the Jews in the relation with Abraham, he sees in Moses a supranational prophet, the master of divine vision and transfiguration."

"That seems orthodox to me, poetic like Islam. But you evaded the question of holy war. And tradition?"

"We can't perpetuate the Middle Ages, that would be going against the spirit of Islam. Each revelation was adapted to the circumstances. We have to imitate the Prophet. Islam instituted neither Church nor clergy; we ourselves have created the chains of tradition, named scholars in order to teach us the Koran. The Prophet himself said: 'The scholars are what is the most virtuous when they are virtuous, and what is the most corrupt when they are corrupt.' I think they're often corrupt. God's people are all of humanity."

Fakhr-el-Nissa doesn't joke. She loves Islam. The contact with the West makes her feel its beauty at the same time as a need for its renewal. Islam, which means abandoning oneself to God, must transfigure man, exalt the best in him, show the action of a transcendent force in his life.

As for Hussein, he doesn't believe in Islam; he claims to be an atheist. But he is an aesthete, bourgeois in spite of himself, ready to love beauty even in religion.

Fakhr-el-Nissa paints; she paints what Layla tells her about: Gamila, her body shrouded in her black sheet, in her arms, a child tormented by flies. She chooses dark colors; her tortured portraits are images of Egypt through the Egyptian woman. Hussein finds that morbid.

"So do Layla's portrait," he jokes, "she resembles a mummy who's come back to life."

"Me," she retorts, "I can see you quite well as the god Bes, the dwarf who makes the gods laugh and the demons flee. He's hideous and indecent."

"Oh!" says Hussein with his big laugh, "I think he's marvelous."

"Do you know," says Layla, "that my name is Wissa and that

that's a deformation of the word Bes? I'm going to say my whole name such as it derives from the genealogical tree of my village: Layla Morcos Wissa Ebeid Wissa Morcos Akhnoukh El-Zordogui ... At home there's a dwarf named Thursday, Khamis. He claims to belong to a family as old as Egypt."

Fakhr-el-Nissa ended up doing Layla's portrait: it resembles the heads found on Coptic cloth, the heads that bordered shrouds during the first centuries of the Church.

The world of political involvement separated Layla from her friends. She liked the life offered to her abroad, and she didn't want to change it. Politics bored her. She didn't understand how her friends could be stirred by the sound of words as dry and ugly as "capitalism,""class struggle,""proletarian masses,""marginal labor," "exploitations" ... She understood well, in their generous spirit, what Hussein and Fakhr-el-Nissan wanted to change, but she discerned poorly the link between abstract words and the misery of the poor. She found it ridiculous that they fought over the newspapers, glued themselves to the radio in order to hear questionable news.

At the Sorbonne, the Communists and the Catholics were fighting for power. Sometimes, one or another of them would be interested in her and would propose various activities, like the pilgrimage to Chartres or discussions about Marx and Hegel. She didn't distinguish clearly between political sides; she liked people and ideas.

Blessed time! The earth belonged to her; her passport gave her the illusion that she could cross all borders. She traveled a lot, often by foot, with her backpack. When Layla was resting under a tree, looking at the sky and the clouds through the branches, she would stop thinking.

In 1948, when the first war in Palestine broke out, all of Layla's circle of friends became restless. Fakhr-el-Nissa feared a new Ulster and denounced the danger of fanatic Zionism. Hussein feared a trap set by King Farouk: wasn't he trying to turn outward the energy of a people in revolution? Madam Morcos was worried and waited anxiously for news and mail.

Layla understood nothing about the problem of Israel; her Jewish friends cared about it even less. They felt differently than other Frenchmen because they had suffered more under the German occupation. They had found themselves, Frenchmen, on the side of the winners, denouncing collaborators with more force than others, throwing eggs and rotten tomatoes more passionately at a Furtwaengler. But they were hardly Zionists.

However, a decisive struggle was taking place, which would transform Layla's entire life. Her older brother had left for the war, proud to be an officer with his machine gun and shining helmet. He had discovered the betrayal beneath wheeling-and-dealing and palace intrigues. The helmet didn't protect him and the gun was rusted. Yahia came back from the war ready to cry out: "Down with the king!"

Palestine was divided, thus establishing, with Zionism, Palestinian powerlessness. And terrorism.

In Deir Yassine, all of the villagers were machine-gunned—women, old people, children—they were thrown into wells, dead or alive. And the news reverberated, spread, from mouth to mouth, from heart to heart, from generation to generation. The grandfather said to the little girl: "Let's flee quickly! Before Deir Yassine happens again." And refugees piled into camps. And the Arab brother said to the Palestinian brother: "Stay in the camp, we'll go to war and return your country to you."

But the Jews repeated: "We were persecuted. We'll demand an eye for an eye: man for man, ten for one, one hundred for one, a thousand for one ... We bought the land from rich property owners. Jews will work it."

And the refugees talked about all the suffering on their land, where the blood was flowing, mixing with milk and honey ...

Layla, who was indifferent to the life of States who deceived men and made use of gods, simply took her exams. She was born too late for this to be an achievement: the adventure had become commonplace for an Egyptian woman. So her photo was not published in Cairo's newspapers.

Fakhr-el-Nissa did not care for diplomas. Her ambition was the same as Hussein's: to work for the people.

Layla was not yet aware that a virus was going to gnaw away at her life: hatred. Like her, the Egyptians were unaware of it. She had her studies to worry about, the world to discover, art books, different landscapes; the people had their misery and didn't even know how to hate. Defeat was for the army and the king, for the privileged classes.

In 1950 Israel put into effect the Law of Return, permitting all Jews to join the nascent Zionist State, and forbidding the Arab peasant to live in his home. A new cold monster had been born from too long a persecution. Yet the revealed word says that a new Israel must announce the end of the world!

This State was built with unequaled perseverance and vitality, with Ouzi machine guns, Galil guns, Barak fighter-bombers, Gabriel sea-to-sea missiles, two-story Jericho missiles and nuclear warheads...?

Some Jews continued to believe in an ideal of universality; Hussein, Hanna, Fakhr-el-Nissa, all who had read Marx, Trotsky, Rosa Luxembourg, shared their dream.

CHAPTER 5

Zebeida's Demon

Fakhr-el-Nissa loved the company of men, their conversation, their attention. She allowed herself to be kissed in public, with the more or less clear intention of playing the game of the emancipated woman, but she abruptly slammed the door in the face of those who asked for more. Some men viewed Fakhr-el-Nissa as coquettish, petty, bourgeoise, and they pretended to no longer know her. Others, attracted by her charm, continued to come to the house as they fussed around one or another of her female friends.

Thus Layla sometimes inherited some of Fakhr-el-Nissa's suitors; Coptic, orthodox and puritanical, she saw herself as greatly honoring a young man by daring to go out with him. She would wear a soft porcupine fur to keep him at elbow's length.

One day Fakhr-el-Nissa met Moustapha at Capoulade's, and she liked him.

"You're afraid of nothing," he said to her. "You must teach the women of Egypt to stand up to men and their laws."

Fakhr-el-Nissa pursed her lips with determination, and said that such was her intention, but that alone she was nothing more than a wisp of straw. So Moustapha proposed that she become a member of the Communist Party. Why hadn't Hussein thought of that?

They took political science classes together, but with the approach of exams, Fakhr-el-Nissa preferred to return to Cairo, paint landscapes and fix misery on her canvasses, dissolve it, dominate it or transform it with lines and colors, but also to search for political expression and religious freedom.

On the quays of the Seine, Moustapha and Fakhr-el-Nissa had seen young people, the retired elderly, the birds and the fish, making love to each other. One Saturday afternoon while they were strolling and talking as usual, they secretly wished to make love to each other. Their conversation continued, and led them to the banks of the Marne, where they had dinner in a dance hall to the sound of an accordion. And so why not spend the night in a hotel and take a boat the next day, with a salami, a camembert and a liter of red wine? With armfuls of lilacs, they returned to Paris late Sunday night, drunken on air, joy and future projects.

After Layla had finished her Bachelor's degree, Madam Morcos decided that it was time to return to Egypt. Did she want to remove her daughter from Hussein's influence? Did she wish to marry her daughter to a Copt? Perhaps she simply wanted to see her house again after three long years of absence.

Madam Morcos kept her moderately priced Parisian apartment, thus avoiding all feelings of rupture. The departure was made easier.

On the boat, Layla leaned on the railing for hours, being tossed about, contemplating the foam of the waves. She became drunk on air and water, dreaming about the delights awaiting her in her country: sun, idleness, hospitality.

In this state of mind she landed in Alexandria. The porters' quarrels and the vulgarities they exchanged shocked her, and, too, the sick eyes of the children fallen prey to the flies. How could Fakhr-el-Nissa give beauty to these miseries?

She walked in the streets and found the city extremely ugly: a false West, false Hellenism, the vanity of the colonized rich. In the past, she had loved the cafés on the coast road, the elegance of the Ramleh trams. Three years spent abroad had spoiled these little joys. She loved the West too much to tolerate the imitation, and loved Egypt too much to accept seeing it crumble under the work of forgerers.

Layla began to hate Alexandria, and she dragged away Madam Morcos, who would have liked to linger by the sea and arouse old memories. On the way to Cairo, the monotony of the countryside delighted her, like a Bach fugue, like the Gregorian masses at the Solesmes Abbey. She was sensitive to the minute variations, to the feeling of the infinite that the repetition of subtle differences expressed. Then there were the pyramids, the narrow green edge of the Nile, the miraculous limits of the desert, the groups of tourists, the camels, the tour guides. Finally, the big house in Rodah, sad and sorry under the dust covers; the beautiful Persian rugs, decomposed by the heat, had disintegrated into clouds of gray dust.

Outside, the crowd and the noise had swelled as if to give them a hostile greeting. With the rise of the Nile, the sewers were over-flowing. A deafening pump was trying to protect the dwelling from a tidal wave of debris. On the pretty Northern Mamelouks Square, there was a bus station, taxis waiting, a garage full of smashed car bodies piled up. A police station was now installed in the beautiful house with the pink marble staircase, built in times past by the Councilor of State. Even the one-eyed street lamp had lost its romantic feeling.

Madam Morcos regretted being required to live, because of her modest fortune, in a neighborhood that was each day turning into more of a slum, but her sadness didn't last. She still kept the hard and solid feeling of superiority, lined as if with a coat of mail, that "well-born" people feel, the certainty of her great moral superiority, the nonetheless large moral superiority of the family, the clan. Little by little, she got over the shock of this first contact. At dawn, the birds were singing as before; the broad bean merchant went by with his big steaming urn. Kawthar had given birth to a beautiful boy, Haroun, who told pretty stories to the birds perched in the trees. He was a big baby, born at the desired time, after his father's medical studies, the official consummation of the marriage and a year-long stay in the United States.

There was also the scribe, in Hour, who did the accounting with the peasants—may God protect him! They'd telephone him, he'd put money in the bank; maybe he himself would come to Cairo with Khamis the dwarf and Wahba the fool. They would buy a new Persian rug for the sitting room, an authentic Boukhara.

Layla saw her dear Zebeida again, made-up, simpering, her hands, feet and hair reddened by henna.

"The damage caused by the change of life," explained Madam Morcos to her sister as she pulled on her needle. And she added with pride:

"I didn't feel the years go by."

She rehired Zebeida— still tortured by her daughter's unhappiness—and tried to reason with her. But the devil was stronger than Madam Morcos. Zebeida was ruining herself financially in order to have herself exorcised. She had already sold her bracelets, her necklace, her gold earrings. Now she had to sacrifice an animal so as to free herself: a cock, maybe a camel. A camel! Madam Morcos shouted loudly. It was one thing to kill a rooster, but she didn't want to hear talk of a camel.

Gamila had resigned herself to living in the shadow of her husband's new spouse—younger, more fortunate and mother of a beautiful baby boy. Hagg Sayed—he was called hagg since he had traveled to Mecca—still poured attention on her—he was a good man—but he gave all of his joy and pride to the new wife who had finally assured him immortality through a true lineage.

Fakhr-el-Nissa explained to Layla that everything would change with Communism, that equality between men and women would be achieved, and that there would be enlightenment for all. Layla listened to her as a child would a lullaby.

She was, in fact, disillusioned. She had believed that the country of her birth would give her an exceptional welcome home. Hadn't she landed herself a philosophy degree at the Sorbonne? Alas, people were particularly sensitive to appearances, and she hadn't learned to care for her own. So what had she gone to do in Paris? She thought she would find once again her joyous circle of school friends, but her girlfriends had to worry about their families. Her cousins were wandering all over the world, or putting on the portliness that comes with high positions.

Surrounded by an excess of family warmth, she felt alone. She was afraid that their concern would smother her.

In the spring and fall, far away near Meadi and Hilwan, she saw nets set out to trap quails. She didn't go near out of fear of seeing the birds caught by their feet in the tight weave, ready to be put in a cage and sold alive. The quails reminded her too much of her own situation as a prisoner.

She questioned the stones. She had a multiple legacy to pass on. At the entrance of Old Cairo, the El-Amr mosque reminded her of how her Coptic ancestors had opened their doors wide to the Moslem conqueror in order to liberate themselves from the yoke of the Byzantines. A few steps from there, the Ben Ezra synagogue blended into the background of this old Christian world. Did the synagogue rise up in the same place where Moses had meditated upon the Exodus? Elsewhere were the Greek gods—Dionysus, Apollo, Hermes—who were repeats of the Egyptian gods …

She would like to have been a painter like Fakhr-el-Nissa, so as to transform all of this heritage into colors, into sketches, perhaps into works of art. She would have painted images of mourning and images of joy, the Palm Sunday crowds, with the blaze of sumptuously woven palm garlands, decorated with flowers and holy bread; the Holy Friday crowd at the hour when Christ's death is announced, when the whole audience makes the sign of the cross and chants one hundred times on each side of the cross: "Kyrie Eleison, Kyrie Eleison, Kyrie Eleison" in a musical phrase of piercing monotony. She would have painted the late meals, sensually devoured after the fast accompanying the slow agony of Christ. The steaming lentil soup was as good as the bread and wine of Communion in the incense vapors …

She felt threatened. This tall handsome priest, in his robe embroidered with a magnificent Coptic cross, who was always asking her the names of her parents, her uncles and aunts, for more assuredness, before giving her absolution, wasn't he going to ask to come and bless the house and burn incense there, a pious pretext masking his desire to get her married?

Certainly, her mother was too suspicious of the priest to finance his matrimonial schemes and send him off to search for a suitor. But there were also society women, all of those patronesses who looked at Layla out of the corners of their eyes and weighed her worth, attentive to the cut of her dress, the quality of her shoes and her handbag, her hairstyle. They discreetly inquired about how many acres of land she possessed and her bank account ...

Under the scrutiny of the priest and the old women, Layla felt like a quail caught in a net.

Life seemed to be on the verge of abandoning her.

For a short time, the idea of suicide occurred to her when she began to weigh all that she would have to erase in order to free herself: her attachment to her family, to the community, her former friendships, a whole mode of existence. She was frightened by the immensity of the mourning she would have to bear.

The idea of death dissipated into romanticism. She camped on the beach in Ein Sokhna, where the coral reefs are high enough to stop sharks, yet let through dangerous barracudas.

Nobody had told her that barracudas, hunting in groups, harass their victims in the same way as men do. She wore her goggles so she could see, in the depths, a dance of multicolored forms and fish who loved and tore each other up, in a world similar to her own, but new, fantastic. A world of colors and clearness. At the edge of the desert, which simulates death, in the clear blue or green of the sea, she dreamed of life.

At night, when the moon was fullest, she would dive again; its reflections on her body, floating just above the water, made of her a being of light.

Dolphins, man's friends, are there to protect her. Layla sees them when she sinks into her sleeping bag, almost at the edge of the water and the sand. They parade by her, the largest in front, the smallest behind, forming large curved shapes with their proud fins, cutting into the waves with dignity, as silent as the starry splendor stretched above them.

One night like that one, Layla had a dream. She was speaking with Hussein; she was telling him that on the beach running next to the desert, there was all of the sand she carried on her that day of Khamsin, when she had met him for the first time. She was also saying to him that the two of them could marry like two stars at the bottom of the sea. Without answering, Hussein, dressed in the traditional caftan, went by, standing on a flying carpet. He was playing the naï[1]; then suddenly he curled up so he could imitate a deformed dwarf and proclaimed in his big voice: "I am Bes, the grotesque god. Do you know me? I preside over celebrations and chase away evil spirits!"

Upon awakening, she had only one wish: to leave.

Layla didn't have the glorious body that could make up for the absence of a father and a fortune.

"Your daughter doesn't know how to dress ... Teach her how to put on make-up. There are cosmeticians ... She has the earthy complexion of the peasant women of Hour. Get her to take care of herself. How do you expect her to marry? You'd think she were a hedgehog!"

Layla saw that glorious body that she was missing, the smooth skin, hairless, in Semiramis, in Shepherds Hotel, at the Inn of the Pyramids; in dresses laminated or embroidered with pearls, a blossoming, arrogant bosom ... Holding the arm of a paunchy consul, minister, judge or councilor. In truth, a glorious body, a mobile fortune, was jealously protected so as to better serve pot-bellied men equipped with a fat wallet.

Layla didn't feel envious. All she wanted was a love story.

"Don't leave right away," Zebeida said to her.

Every morning, she turned over her cup of Turkish coffee onto the little saucer, and in the images of the coffee grounds, read her future to her: "Your heart is heavy, full of worries, but don't let it overwhelm you. Look at this beautiful fish: happiness is going to fall from the sky for you ... There's a big black cloud near the handle of the cup, but don't be discouraged; I see a large door opening ..."

Layla watches intently, each month, the moon's crescent. She sings a poem to her: "Shine, blessed moon. Fill our eyes with your light and our hands with your happiness."

Innumerable months have gone by, and nothing has changed. She

---

[1] Naï: a reed pipe.

watches, she hunts for a look filled with the hope promised by the moon.

On January 26, 1952, from the top floor of a house in Zamalek, Layla saw Cairo in flames. Nothing was happening in the old city, nor in the neighborhood of the Egyptian museum. The places she loved seemed to be spared; it was the commercial center of Cairo that was burning. Layla found the spectacle quite beautiful.

Cabarets, luxury cinemas, large hotels, the Barclay Bank, Groppi, the Swiss pastry shop, the Turf Club, the department stores belonging to the Jewish upper middle class—Cicurel, Chemla, Adès—all had been burned. Palestine had just been defeated by a young Israel. Was all of the old world going to burn?

That morning, workers and civil servants had gone into the streets demanding extreme measures from the politicians; asking them to arm the people, to organize the national resistance. In the evening, the masses, who did not belong to these respectable classes, without waiting, had begun to burn and ransack.

There were massacres. With his big paunch and sunglasses, the king did not forsake his calmness; he continued to covet the glorious bodies that the fire had not frightened to death, bodies that would not delay in finding other big hotels and other fashionable cabarets to exhibit themselves in.

Layla had hoped for a moment that the popular tide would sweep away the paunchy men, the glorious bodies and a few other sacrosanct values. Like Zebeida, she felt possessed by a demon, a demon that only fire could exorcise.

But her mother could not offer her fire anymore than she could procure a camel for Zebeida. There was nothing left for her other than to go abroad.

Seven years—during which Egypt would chase out its pot-bellied king and bring into power the humiliated soldiers of 1948—seven years of abundance. Layla spends them preparing theses at the university. With the pretext of research, she spends a lot of time in Oxford, Cambridge and London.

tense ?

But because she feels nostalgia for the desert, as soon as she goes away, she repeatedly returns to Egypt. If she sees the crowd again swelling around her house in Rodah, the clicking noises of the pump and the hiccuping of the sewers on Northern Mamelouks Square becoming more and more intolerable, poor Zebeida's misery growing with her daughter's, she shares, on the other hand, the great hope for the revolution which consoles her great despair for the fire that had missed its goal.

Some of her cousins introduce her into new circles of friends; she discovers an Arab world that she was unaware of, learns to handle the different dialects, savors the words, the mixing of languages.

She also learns to make herself discreet, mysterious, desirable perhaps, without letting anyone guess her blind attachment to Hussein, whom she suspects is in love with a young Englishwoman whose mother is Italian. In order to hide her disappointment, she pretends that she's had great love affairs with handsome strangers, and is almost convinced by her own game.

One carnival day, she disguises herself as an Egyptian peasant. Hussein doesn't let anyone else dance with her. She feels beautiful: with the costume she borrowed the haughty look of the peasant woman. Layla discovers that her eyes are shaped for the coquetry of the veil and its falsely shameful audacity. She dares to seduce.

Her friends are amused to see her brushing the cobwebs off herself and keeping a calendar full of rendezvous with admirers. They pester her with questions: Has she found her prince charming? What country is he from? Layla says that she loves too many of them and doesn't know which one to choose. Does she believe in free love? Hussein, a bit embarrassed, laughs; curious, he waits for an answer, a glint of desire in her eye. Layla, in her turn, threatens to be indiscreet. Hussein pretends to be serious:

"Young women," he pompously declares, "must remain virgins until the day of their marriage."

Is he really joking? Torn between two contradictory sets of morals, Layla decides to do what she wants and keep it a secret.

It is considered fashionable manners, in certain rich milieus of Cairo, to have a choice of lovers. "What, she's a virgin? Such a little bourgeoise!" people would say with slight contempt. However, at the same time, people are not kind toward "liberated" intellectual women. "Badly dressed, false women!" They're not envied any more than the young provincial women, shut between the four walls of their homes, private property of a father or a prospective husband.

Indeed, the Egyptian woman, whatever she does, is always eaten alive! Layla gives no one the chance to judge her. She allows a comfortable doubt to surround her love life.

One August in Alexandria, Fakhr-el-Nissa married, without any fanfare, without preparing a trousseau or furnishing a house. She and Moustapha preferred to buy each chair, each pot, according to their whim. They flouted the Moslem custom which demands that the wife provide everything while the husband provides just the lights. In truth, the custom has lost its poetic quality: since the arrival of technology, the husband must bring, along with the lights, all of the household appliances.

In Paris, Oxford and Cambridge, the thesis writers are busy doing their work. Some of them have gone as far as Harvard or California.

Zebeida was wasting away under the burden of illness and poverty, sucked to the marrow by her "demon."

Her daughter Gamila had demanded a divorce, and her husband had accepted. She had even obtained a comfortable monthly pension. In order to increase her earnings, she chose to sell oranges. With a basket on her head, she roamed the streets of Rodah or Old Cairo, singing the praises of her merchandise to the tune of a mournful and monotonous chant: "Honey, my oranges, a piastre for a wekkah[2] of oranges…"

To rest her voice and feet, she mixed in with circles of women and workers in the populous neighborhoods. The heat of the street provided her with a sort of happiness. She prostituted herself a bit, more for the pleasure than for the money.

---

[2] Wekkah: slightly over a kilo in weight. A term no longer in use.

Her mother moaned a lot. She spoke despairingly and with volubility of the demon inhabiting Gamila. But she didn't forget her own.

CHAPTER 6
Goha's Nail

O ne spring, Layla successfully defended her doctoral thesis in philosophy. She was pondering the best way to begin a new phase of her life when, on July 26, 1956 ... Nasser, a Saïdi like herself, originally from a village in Upper Egypt called Beni-Mor, made a historical decision.

In the heart of an Alexandria drunken on sun, he announced that he was going to nationalize the Suez Canal Company.

"You can't stay in Europe," some of Layla's friends said to her. "There's going to be war."

"What an absurd idea!" said Layla.

"Why leave?" said another. "After all, you're an expatriate."

The word hurt her. Expatriate, with her ancestors, her face, that feeling of being Egyptian right down to her bones?

The owner of her apartment, convinced that those Egyptian troublemakers in Algeria, dishonest to boot with their story of nationalizing the canal, were finally going to be made to see reason, demanded the immediate termination of her rental contract.

Layla finally embarked for Egypt.

During the crossing, she felt revitalized by nationalistic pride. Egypt was at last taking its destiny into its own hands. The British and French had removed their pilots from the canal, believing they could thus create an inextricable situation; but a handful of Egyptians, taking up the challenge, had just shown what this unrecognized people could do. The canal was not blocked. Layla was glued to the news. So, she noticed with surprise, politics did concern her.

The revenue from the canal would be used to finance the dam

that Foster Dulles refused to give to Egypt. Egyptian students from all corners of the world returned home to participate in the construction of their country.

Nasser was a great man for all!

To go from Alexandria to Cairo, Layla chose, instead of the usual desert route, that of the countryside, because in the month of September the cotton flower covers the country with its exuberant beauty. Everything is filled with diaphanous white flowers. People sing the praises of cotton as if it were a pretty girl, as if the sun were not beaming down its pitiless rays on the backs of the workers. Added to the joy of the harvest that year was the confidence born of a young revolution that was finally giving to each peasant the hope of one day cultivating his own earth.

Except for that, nothing had changed. Dismal and noisy life continued in the villages. For drinking, bathing, and doing their laundry, the peasants still preferred the red silt-laden water of the canals to clear fountain water. The flies must belong to another generation of flies, but they strangely resembled those Layla had left behind on children's eyes, in the corner grocer's stall. The cicadas still droned their impressive chorus of heat and wind. Naked feet still ran on the scorching road to lighten its burn.

For a few weeks in Cairo, Layla looked for work and found none. At the university and in the secondary schools, all of the philosophy posts were occupied by French, British or Egyptian professors.

Hussein and Moustapha taught at the university. Fakhr-el-Nissa was accumulating victories: political action, painting, she succeeded in everything. Her name was becoming famous, and Layla was very proud of her friend; she liked to accompany her on her excursions to the countryside, or to feminist meetings, and to participate in her discussions with women from all walks of life, while drinking mint tea or eating lamb kebabs.

Hussein proposed to teach Layla how to drive. He took her out of the city, into the desert or onto country roads. Their hands met on the steering wheel, their cheeks brushed each other's ...

A gamousse wanted to cross the road. "Put on the brakes!" cried out Hussein. Layla accelerated ... The windshield shattered. The car buckled with a very loud sound. The poor beast had a broken paw, a big gamousse paw. The fellah accompanying it was in despair. A crowd gathered around the accident. A *chaouiche* arrived from the neighboring village: a real gentleman with his white uniform, his silver plated buttons, his wide belt, his big cane. With great authority, he reprimanded the fellah. How could one think of allowing animals to wander on the road! The country will never make any progress as long as there are such ignorant peasants ... He pocketed the pound note that Hussein discreetly slipped to him, checked the condition of the car, and watched it drive off.

Hussein invited Layla to recover from her upset on the patio of the Sémiramis Hotel. They watched the bridges open up before the white sails of the majestic feluccas passing by. Hussein listed the marvels promised by the revolution.

"Will they slaughter the gamousse?" asked Layla worriedly.

"There will be," insisted Hussein, "insurance for animals and for the peasant reliant on their work. Egypt is well on the way to solving all of these problems. Everything is slowly but surely moving forward ..."

Hussein continued giving driving lessons to Layla ... In a village, he saw a veiled peasant woman go by. Eastern tradition demanded that he pay her homage. He stuck his head out of the car window and cried out:

"Show what you're hiding, my beauty!"

In the wink of an eye, men brandishing their fearsome staffs and the *nabbout* came out from everywhere, ready to leap onto Hussein and beat him up.

Hussein put up the car windows, took Layla's place at the steering wheel, and raced off, followed by a procession of angry men, their moustaches hopping madly, their robes puffed out by the wind.

Sheltered by the shaded streets of Cairo, Layla and Hussein laughed like children who have just escaped a beating. They stopped at the tip of the island under the flame trees. They kissed for a long time. A chaouiche came by.

"That's forbidden, Mister Bey, I have to take you to the police station."

Hussein gave him a tip.

"Okay," said the chaouiche. "But be careful, or else you'll send me to the devil. We're poor people, Mister Bey!"

Hussein took Layla to visit the new oil refineries, the weaving factories, and the first agricultural cooperatives. Egypt was going to begin a new era.

Would Hussein ask Layla to marry him?

Power was in the hands of intelligent people, of young officers in the wind of hope. Yehia, Layla's brother who was already a major, was one of them, with an arrogant eagle on the epaulette of his uniform.

They wanted to sweep away the artificial elite that had exploited the country. They had the power to gag the sanctimonious and the fanatics, to dismantle, for example, the organization of the Moslem Brotherhood. They were courageously preparing to abolish the idea of a state religion, and to symbolize this liberating gesture, they had taken the giant statue of Ramses out of his bed of sand, in the heart of a palm grove, and solemnly installed him on the square in front of the train station, right in the middle of the bustling crowd. Beyond the era of Christian Egypt, it was that of the pharaohs they wanted to call upon in order to teach grandeur to this crowd.

Layla, Hussein, Moustapha, and their friends had turned against their fathers, their elderly aunts, their ancestors; they were all in the same boat, those who had adapted themselves to a rotten world, and those who had tried, painfully, to live honestly.

The older people of their milieu, for the most part dispossessed of their land and buildings, predicted great misfortunes.

"Lamenting consoles them," mocked the young people.

"Agrarian reform is a utopia," preached an old uncle. "There will never be enough land in Egypt for all of the peasants. The yield will be disastrous."

"He's crying over his lost feddans," commented the new generation, "and the serfs he can no longer exploit!"

After all, it was the idea of a genius to nationalize the canal. All Nasser had done was to take possession again of a national resource being exploited by foreigners. So who could find fault in that? But the anger of the great powers fell on the land of Egypt, and the national resource served no one.

The great powers spoke at length about their good feelings and about the support necessary for underdeveloped countries. It wasn't against Egypt that they held a grudge; they had always wanted to help her. But Nasser! Nasser was a tyrant from whom it was urgent to save the Egyptian people in order to rediscover the former Egypt, a country blessed by the gods.

If they had left Nasser to do as he wished, Layla sometimes thought, perhaps he would have succeeded in building a powerful Egypt, in transforming the national character, in giving pride to men who did not feel they were born for grandeur.

Had he been less hunted down, wouldn't he have acted more humanely? The terrified faces around him had to cover themselves with a comedian's mask, similar to those that the monkey-trainer exhibits in the streets of Cairo ... Layla asked herself the question: would the *Rayyis* have been what he was if the West had not constantly placed traps and pitfalls in his path?

Much later in 1967, after the Six Day War, a foreign friend of Layla's felt obliged to say to her:

"Console yourself. Good can come from evil. After this defeat you'll be able to rid yourselves of your Hitler."

Something rebelled in her. No, the comparison was not fair. For the first time in thousands of years, a foreigner was not running the country. For the first time in thousands of years, Egypt had an Egyptian Rayyis, a Saïdi, like Hussein, like Fakhr-el-Nissa, like Layla.

The West had sworn his downfall, but for the Egyptians, they associated hope with this tyrant who had become a tyrant in spite of his own will, because of the wicked will of the great powers ...

In the fall of 1956, the anger of the superpowers was let loose:

Israeli tanks rushed through the Sinai Desert toward the canal, a cloud of French and British parachutists descended on Port Saïd and Port Fouad in order to "protect the canal installations."

Were France and England using Israel? Or was it the other way around? Whatever, for the common people, the attack became "the triple and cowardly aggression." The operation was going to succeed, Nasser's regime would undoubtedly collapse, while Russia and America groaned: pipelines were being sabotaged all over the Near East!

For all those who had studied in France and England, countries they had learned to love, consternation and indignation vied with each other. Friends from their prosperous years were sending them bombs! The rancor of these Egyptians equaled their disappointment.

Layla had lost her memories of Paris as the city of lovers. All that remained was the vindictive silhouette of her landlord: "Serves them right! Those Egyptian troublemakers, hypocritical, dishonest!" Pettiness and disenchantment. Layla was even angry with herself for her Parisian manners. Everything she had assimilated from French culture stuck to her skin like the plague, like mange. She began to hate herself.

She took down her grandfather's portrait, the symbol in her eyes of everything, in her, which allied her to the West: her sympathies were now with that Copt, Al Eryan, who had tried to assassinate the old man; she identified with him. She felt so much resentment toward everything that linked her to the West that she forbade herself to pronounce the merest word in French or English, and she began studying Arabic and the Koran with an ardor that could only equal her anger. Her nationalism, born ten years earlier on the quay of the Lyon train station, had painfully matured.

One thought irritated Layla's Coptic soul: that the Jews could be used as a screen, as an alibi, after having seen them, without reacting, rotting in the concentration camps and perishing in crematory ovens. The West was buying back its virgin conscience the easy way.

They were playing dice with the Jew. If he were to win, they would once again be the masters of the Near East. If he were to lose, there would be, in the worst of cases, a new Auschwitz.

But the Western powers didn't have a monopoly on this monstrous Machiavellianism they had thought up, because the Jew, for his part, was using the West in order to meet his goals. State reason, she finally understood, paid no attention to borders. Politics worked everywhere to the sound of the tocsin and the death knell.

Politics was gambling with the Jew as it was with Layla.

She had loved countries other than her own and other gods in a big picture book. She was the heiress of neither a Catholic paradise nor a Moslem paradise. No one religion, no one moral code seemed to her to sum up all of the wisdom of the world. Even her nationalism was never anything but a large wound, the sign of a war within herself. Layla could not entirely place herself in any of the existing camps. Everything was swirling around in her. And this was what was certainly distorting the game, for the chessboard on which she found herself had been designed in black and white squares, without anyone asking Layla her opinion. There wasn't even any gray!

Layla began to frantically read the newspapers in order to catch up on lost time, to find some meaning in the course of events. Perhaps she would get there by piecing the news together? So she allowed herself to be taken in by the game that her friends had been playing already for so many years.

The Rayyis, like Layla, would have preferred to be confined to the gray zone. America forbade him to: America certainly wanted to finance the Assouan dam, and furnish the Egyptian army with all of the necessary gaudy accessories. But a choice was necessary: stand with all of the Middle East on the side of NATO, face a common enemy ... "the Russian enemy?" said the Rayyis, "permit me: our enemy is English." And to make things worse, Britain was a member of NATO.

White square? Black square?

Nasser turned to Moscow. And the Russian bear entered the scene with its paw outstretched, a big good bear paw that had just smashed the Hungarians but now, claws pulled in, was offering treats. The stuff out of which to make the Egyptians good, true Communists.

If it were possible …

Since the "triple and cowardly aggression," the Egyptians had been recounting the story of Goha's nail in order to laugh a bit and relax the atmosphere.

Goha is the hero of innumerable Egyptian tales. Sometimes wise, sometimes crazy, idiotic or malicious, greedy or generous, Goha—a sort of metaphysical clown—gave birth to a myth. He prefers the moon, which offers a little bit of light in the night, to the sun that shines uselessly in the middle of the day …

Here is the story of Goha's nail, such as it was told at the end of the 1956 events:

"One day Goha sells his house. He gets a good price for it. However, he keeps a nail for himself, which is located near the ceiling, above the entryway. Laughing, the new owner happily allows him this innocent fantasy: a nail is worth nothing, right? One year later, Goha comes to visit his nail. For just a moment. But then he comes back a month later, then every day, a little longer each day, then for a day and a night, and every day and every night. Until the owners, exasperated, end up abandoning the whole house to him, with its walls, its furniture, and its nail."

A British Goha with an Israeli nail? The symbol perceived in this absurd story created the illusion that it would be possible to play off the enemy's tricks. The Rayyis was capable of doing this; people had confidence in him. They already had guessed his idea: Arab unity in order to tear out Goha's nail. While waiting, use the nail in order to forge a new will for power. He who laughs last laughs longest.

The story of Goha covered the unpardonable confrontation of Abraham's children with a light veil of humor. But it had a weak point: it deliberately ignored the nature and the importance of the nail: the Jewish determination to construct a State in spite of everything, with the strength derived from prolonged suffering. It forgot the unending battle of Jewish terrorism against the British. Furthermore, Goha was on the verge of giving his nail to the Americans.

In the state of confusion in which she was struggling, Layla, Coptic, Christian, defector from a mythical West, put all of her hope in Hussein's, Moustapha's, and Fakhr-el-Nissa's Marxism, a Marxism disdainful of religious and racial divisions, and the defender of the earth's disinherited.

But the Russian bear was slowly, surely, advancing its huge furry paws. Marxism was transforming itself into a new religion in the service of a temporal power. The entire world was marching together in tight lines, in war herds. Woe to those who wanted to think and understand.

Egyptian intellectuals became all fired up when Arab brothers or an Arab nation were mentioned.

All knew, however, that a common denominator still needed to be invented. Race? Copts repressed by conquest, Moslems with the profile of Akhenaten, the sons of Turks and Circassians to whom the Arab was often an inferior, Lebanese who were proud of their Phoenician ancestors and their cosmopolitan culture, Berbers and Moors; what did all of them have of the Semitic? Language? Arabic permitted communication among the cultivated elite, but a wall of dialect separated the fruit and vegetable merchant of the streets of Paris from the Arabian Bedouin. Islam? Alas, in many cases, it offered nothing but a medieval rut imposed by authoritarian regimes.

But that which made Arabism weak also made it strong. Rather than a reality, it was a beautiful abstraction out of which a myth could emerge, possibly a cause. Abroad, all of the "Arabs" scattered from different parts of the world felt a sense of solidarity, in spite of social differences. A sort of diffuse empathy with each other. Could modern media create this spontaneous rapport for those who had never traveled?

Would the Rayyis, who had known how to quiet the opposition in Egypt, and unite the people under his banner, be able to rally together all of the so-called Arab countries? The intellectuals remained somewhat skeptical.

The working classes did not take seriously the Jewish myth, vital force of the Arab myth, until after the catastrophe of 1967.

The events brought Layla and Hussein closer together. They looked for what might still be salvaged from their years abroad.

Letters reached them from France or England, after having been detoured through Belgium or Italy. Friends were disassociating themselves from the politics of their countries. Layla and Hussein devoured these letters and distributed photocopies of them.

Never had they needed each other so much. Except for religion, which no longer meant much to them, everything brought them together: their family histories resembled each other like those of innumerable Egyptian families. Their mothers were childhood friends. Their fathers came from the same region of Minieh.

They liked to remember the land from which they came.

"I come from the Saïd," said Hussein.

"I'm a Saïdeya," said Layla.

"Spit this word out of your mouth!" exclaimed indignantly a woman dressed in black.

"But," retorted Layla, taken aback, "my father comes from Hour!"

"Say that you own a few acres of 'mud' in the Saïd," groaned the woman as she struck her chest, "but don't say you're a Saïdeya. With your intelligence! Your education!"

Amused, Hussein and Layla collected stories about the people of Saïd, people of the sun, from the South.

"A Saïdy takes the train for Cairo," recounted Layla. "A flea teases him. When they've almost arrived in Cairo, he catches it. The ugly flea! He holds it in his fingers, pondering how he'll take his revenge. 'Am I going to squash you? Torture you? Pull off your legs?' But suddenly, arriving in Cairo, he decides, and delighted, places the insect on the ground. 'You'll walk home!'"

Layla lived comfortably and pampered thanks to the money from the Saïd she had never seen, and for which she felt, all of a sudden, an incomprehensible nostalgia. Twice a year, her father used to go to the village in order to count the produce of the harvest with the peasants. He knew each one of them by name. But Layla, for her part, seemed to have cut the umbilical cord.

Life returned to normal in Cairo. Universities and schools opened their doors once again; the English and French professors left. Layla was called upon from everywhere. She would finally drown her tormented imagination in her work.

She took the place of a French professor at the university. She had to continue his class in French. She struggled for the first two hours; during the third, in spite of herself, the words poured out in Arabic. The Dean understood and excused her. Her students amused themselves teaching her the subtle balance between the spoken language and the pedantry of the written language. It was difficult; she had to take many private lessons.

With Hussein's help, she searched thoroughly into the literary treasures of the Middle Ages to find the necessary words. She breathed new life into them in order to express foreign notions and ideas. She became drunk on words. Later, she participated in the development of a lexicon. Her enthusiasm would then wane, because the words had to be simplified in order to give them an exact equivalency.

During the following winter she finally realized her dream: to leave for Hour. As the oldest of the family, her brother Yehia accompanied her.

"The village roots," he explained to her, "go back only to the eighteenth century. A Copt who had murdered a Moslem took refuge here and cultivated the land. He was named El-Zordogui, to evoke the rabbit who burrows in his hole."

"Then another important Moslem family settled in the country, but the descendants of El-Zordogui remained the mayors for generations by right of seniority. The memory of the two families, one Coptic, the other Moslem, still haunts the village. As for the memory of Heket the Frog, goddess of these places, for ages she has been buried in books or forgotten on sarcophagi, or on the sides of earthenware lamps. However, the frog, like the sun, symbolizes the breath of life, renewal. Without her, the potter god Khnoum, who made man on his wheel, would perhaps have only invented inert creatures. Without her, Osiris would perhaps have been only the god of death. The first

Christians, who designed a frog to represent resurrection, knew this."

Layla and her brother arrived in Hour on the first day of the month of Amchir, the coldest of the Coptic calendar. In Upper Egypt, the rhythm of the seasons and harvests is still measured in ancient terms.

Hour resembles a thousand other villages. On a first level, there are earth-colored houses with flat roofs; higher up is a mosque pointing its minaret to the sky, a church wearing its cross on an impressive dome, and a pigeon roost made of earthenware jugs with holes in the bottom. Groves of palm trees spread out their branches on the heights of the village, as if to say to the minaret and the cross: "We are the most ancient, like Egypt, we are eternal. You are a luxury; we are absolutely necessary to life. The Mesopotamians were already chanting our three hundred sixty uses! Our branches filter the sun, our fruit feeds men. Without us, people here wouldn't know what drunkenness is."

A delegation of cousins, the dwarf Khamis, and Wahba the fool were waiting for the travelers at the train station. Yehia was greeted with wide-open arms, a slap on the back and a handshake, and then the greetings began all over again. Layla felt great joy at finding her friends again.

They went in a procession to the home of the 'omdeh (the mayor). Renaissance style, tall windows and high ceilings. No garden separated it from the peasant homes surrounding and protecting it from all sides. This is because the land of Saïd is not always very safe: the people easily take justice into their own hands. Woe to the owner who didn't want to rent his land, the father who refused his daughter in marriage, the crazy man who deflowered an adolescent girl: honor is avenged promptly and discreetly with a knife stab.

The 'omdeh wasn't there: he was busy with the festivities of his own marriage taking place in the neighboring town, Minieh. In order to receive Layla, a large wing of the house was cleaned and the water mill was put into operation (the generator was out of order).

The meal was served at a cousin's house. All of the various meats from the area except for pork, prohibited since ancient times (pork is impure, the pig never lifts its head to the sky), were spread out on the table. There were whole ducks, stuffed pigeons, roasted chickens, boiled rabbit, a leg of lamb to modestly represent the lamb, a ragout to show that beef had been thought of, slices of veal. Grape leaves, zucchinis and eggplants were stuffed with more meat.

The cousin, dressed in a long robe with wide sleeves, presided over the table, carved the leg of lamb and the chickens with his big generous hands, offered the best pieces, invoked the dead and the living god so that the guests would very much want to eat more. In Madam Morcos's home, this kind of profusion of dishes, covering the peasant tables, was always viewed with some scorn, but Layla savored, without prejudice, this hospitality, and she regretted that her stomach had become so small from eating a Western diet.

She would like to have spoken with her brother and cousin about horses, cultivation, and the cotton worm, but she had to respect custom, sit with the women, admire her cousin's wardrobe: drapes and flounces, pink taffetas and blue satins.

"It's the fashion in Paris," said her cousin. "Priceless material bought in the city."

Layla felt uneasy. She had come to see an almost timeless village. The Coca-Cola ads at the train station, the Renaissance family home, her cousin's wardrobe, seemed to disagreeably trouble the immobility of the centuries.

She went and consoled herself in her grandmother's old abandoned house. There was a large courtyard surrounded by reception rooms, overhung by a square gallery that let in the sky and the sun. The bedrooms, looking out onto the gallery, were next to vast rooms used for storing rice, barley, beans; a room for each kind of grain, with a trap door opening toward the floor, both for pouring and for letting in air. In her grandparents' time, these grains were used as monetary exchange. They were bartered for zucchinis, onions, garlic, dried dates, all of the peasant's fortune. Layla had heard that her grandfather's second wife, still a young bride, had been found buried, smothered in the courtyard under the weight of the beans that had cascaded out because of a trap door carelessly left open. Layla's grandmother, her grandfather's third wife, had not wanted to live there. That's when they had built the solid Renaissance-style house which had become the family home, with no interior courtyard, no grain storage rooms, separated from the sky and the sun by its high walls.

Layla went to visit Khamis at his home. The dwarf's sister prepared some *betaoui*, a light and crusty bread made of corn flour and fenugreek. They sat at a round table, broke the bread apart, dipped it into a green soup, and shared a chicken.

Khamis told Layla what had happened to her grandparents:

"Your grandfather had money to buy some new land. The deal had been made when the thieves came … Thieves? In reality, they were peasants who were cultivating the land and were threatened with losing it. During the night they came in, their faces hidden under big shawls. There were twenty of them, with revolvers. Your grandfather had to give them the money … He knew the thieves, but he didn't dare denounce them for fear they would take revenge on his children. He died shortly afterward. Your grandmother went insane. May God rest her soul!"

"And you, Khamis," asked Layla, "you live apart. Aren't you afraid?"

"We're poor. We live from one day to the next on sales of giblets and the cultivation of a bit of land. We're dwarfs, but we're taken for goblins. People leave us alone."

Layla told Khamis that she wanted to return to the village to start a sacred theater. The dwarf pretended to be enthusiastic, but he wasn't very convinced. They continued their talk in the foul-smelling odor of the house. The women listened silently. Outside, the sky was slowly devouring the sun. There were nothing but fields in front of Khamis's house, a huge checkerboard cut across by channels, earth levees opened up with a hoe to let the water run through. In the distance, against the blaze of the setting sun, the women were returning home, jugs on their heads, tall black silhouettes stirring up clouds of dust with their long dresses, as if to erase their footprints.

The land was not encumbered by fences; there was no barbed wire separating individual property. A little dwarf, lantern in hand, accompanied a young woman who had come from the city through the fields. The peasants they ran into, gathered around fires, made gestures imprinted with ancestral dignity. They lived intimately with the land they watched over twelve months of the year. A pickle was enough for them to eat with their bread. An onion was a feast. "You can leave for the city," they seemed to be saying. "Go on, we'll take care of your land. You don't need to get your hands dirty. You can look disgusted when you smell the odor of the manure that feeds our fire, enriches the mud, perfumes the very bread that we eat. We are the masters of the earth because we belong to it."

The dwarf accompanied the young woman all the way to the mayor's house. Leading her through long corridors, he set the lantern down on the table, and left in the dark, to go find again the hovel where the female dwarfs had spread out their mats close to the stove, as they prepared to sleep next to a family of goats.

Khamis took off his *babouches* and his caftan, worn only on feast days; he huddled in a corner of the hearth and waited for sleep to come. The light of the day no longer required that he laugh and make others laugh. Khamis thought about the hen he had killed in order to offer a sumptuous meal to the young city woman, of the money needed to pay for the farm rent and the seeds. He hoped and despaired. He wouldn't be sent away from his land; the revolution, henceforth, would protect him. Still, one has to live … His sister spoke softly to him during the night: His daughter was gone for many hours; a certain Yassin often passed by the house. Not far off, the sugar cane was already getting tall. Did she leave to go and make love like the goats? Misfortune! The sons of evil are innumerable. But his daughter was a dwarf: a normal man would never marry her … Khamis had stopped laughing. He was dreaming, melancholy, about everything that caused his melancholy.

As for Layla, she was settling into an imaginary world, happy about so much beauty, saddened by the slow death of an entire past, vaguely conscious of all the misery surrounding her. Outside, in the light of the moon, a naï player lengthened his song—in order to exorcise evil spirits? A woman intoned a chant, a *mawal*, a poem:

"Tell me, Baheya, who killed Yassin?"

Layla fell asleep and dreamed that Khamis had killed a man. She woke up with a start. It was eleven o'clock; the night threatened to be long. She relit the lantern and wandered around the house: immense hallways, rooms leading one into the other, white dust covers, dust, big chandeliers, broken toilet flushers, piles of empty boxes in the wardrobes, bundles beneath the sofas. Maybe, one day, she would have enough money to buy the whole abandoned lot.

Would she establish a sacred theater, a cultural center? For five days, she would be a privileged tourist, able to philosophize in Arabic with the boatman or the taxi driver. She would traverse the region in all directions, visit the temples and the monasteries. Would she be able, one day, to let her friends, on the other side of the ocean, know of these finds?

The Tell-el-Amarna ruins were close by, laden with the memory of their pharaoh Akhenaten. Layla held him responsible for the ravages of Near Eastern monotheism. The first prophet of internationalism, the first "individual" of the universe? Or its first fanatic? A man who preached love for all men and, like all men, didn't at all know how to love? The inventor of a single spiritual God or the simple interpreter of a latent monotheism? A castrated man, a demeaned man, or a great thinker who forbade the representation of sex in sculptures in order to express a theological vision of the world: eternal life before birth, life and death were differentiated?

Layla went back to bed. In order to fall asleep, she read Moses, by Freud: Moses has the same name as the pharaohs—Ah-mose, Thout-mose, Râ-mose; an abandoned child, who came into the world against the will of the father, an Egyptian prince from the epoch of Akhenaten; he practiced the monotheism of the latter or at least knew Aton's doctrines. Egyptologist friends of Layla's agreed however that Moses lived after Akhenaten, perhaps during the epoch of Ramses II, and that the Hebrews were made up of bands of Hapirou mercenaries. Would she attack Freud's translation or put together herself a new story?

In the library of the Museum of Alexandria, she had read the hymns of Akhenaten and the psalms of David; their similarity had struck her. How can a people separate itself from another people, a religion from another religion, and how can the clash of small differences create an explosive situation that threatens the entire world?

The hours went by and still Layla could not fall back asleep. A round of new ideas, of crazy ideas, turned in her head.

She remembered that Hour is on the edge of Bahr-el-Youssoufi, the "sea of Joseph," a canal that Joseph, according to the legend, had dug and whose course he traced with the end of his cane. Today, still, some speak of "pharaoh Joseph" in reference to Joseph's well at the summit of Mokattam. Yet the well was built on orders of Saladin—who was called Joseph by the emir Baha-el-Din Qaraqûsh.

A curious destiny, that of Qaraqûsh, thought Layla. He became the prototype of the tyrant with absurd whims, a sort of Egyptian precursor to Ubu-Roi! And only because his name resembled that of the Turkish clown Qaragheuz ... Layla remembered one of the innumerable stories about Qaraqûsh:

One day a thief fell out of a rickety window. He filed a complaint with the governor Qaraqûsh.

"I am a professional thief," he said, "and I demand justice!"

Qaraqûsh had the owner brought forward, who then placed the responsibility for the unstable window on the carpenter. When called in, the carpenter next accused the beauty and the red dress of a young woman, who, passing by in the street, had distracted him from his work. The young woman was brought in, and she defended herself:

"My beauty," she said, "comes from Allah, and my red dress comes from the dyer."

Qaraqûsh had the dyer arrested, and he, stuttering and dazed, wasn't able to place the blame on anyone.

"Have him hanged at the door of the prison," ordered Qaraqûsh.

Unfortunately, the dyer was too tall and the door was too low. It was impossible to hang him. So Qaraqûsh said majestically:

"Go through the city. Find me a small dyer and hang him in his place!"

Layla realized that it was Qaraqûsh, or Qaragheuz, who was

still directing the politics of men today. Full of imperturbable seriousness, the powerful make their prayer: "Abraham, father of all, give us our daily war." And the rich man pushes ahead ultra-modern killing machines. And the poor man, in despair, hides in the bushes, a knife in his hand, to stab the aggressor's back. "How cowardly!" cries out the rich man. "We have to massacre him, him and his cohorts, in order to save civilization!"

Layla had unmasked Qaraqûsh-Qaragheuz long before. For example, he holds up the myth of a Jewish race. "The Jews? People who have roots," Madam Morcos used to say. Strange roots! Moses himself was maybe an Egyptian prince; in the sixth century, a Yemenite prince, Dhou-Nawas, converted to Judaism with all of his subjects. In the Russian steppes certain Khazars followed the same path. So they provide ancestors to today's Israelis! There are even black Jews, so it's said, Cochina China Jews …

For a whole year, Layla tried to rid herself of all that was Western. But the trauma of the war had passed; the fierce nationalism was beginning to cool down in spite of the continuing tension.

Layla decided for herself to no longer follow the orders of Qaraqûsh-Qaragheuz. She had been forbidden to marry Hussein because he was Moslem and she was Coptic. But that was all over with. Layla would disobey. She would marry Hussein …

The big bed, perched between four columns, was cozy and comfortable. Layla fell asleep. Her dream prolonged the crazy round of her ideas.

"Let's recite the lesson," she said to her students. "I am a Coptic pawn, you are a Moslem pawn. I am an Egyptian pawn; you are a Jewish pawn. I am a Russian pawn, you are an American pawn." And Moses?

"And Moses?" asked a student.

"I don't know," said Layla, "maybe he was schizophrenic."

"Who makes pawns work?" asked another student.

"Let's see, let's see!" answered Layla. "So don't you know? It's Qaraqûsh-Qaragheuz!"

"What were you yelling about in your dream?" asked Yehia in the morning. "Can't you sleep like everyone else?"

"I live like everyone," said Layla, "and like everyone else, I have megalomaniac dreams. I dreamed that I was a pawn by myself!"

CHAPTER 7
Prison Shadows

In the old streets of *The Thousand and One Nights*, Layla spoke a lot about Hour. Cairo evenings, and their lightheartedness, gave the poet the illusion of a flying carpet, and inspired in her the nostalgia of a village inhabited by dwarves, gods and demons.

During the summer months, she left again for Hour, still thinking of her sacred theater. She dreamed of the "Recovery of Osiris" or "The Mystery of Horus," performed in the temple of the frog Heket. Her Cairo friends listened to her with tender irony. Ask uneducated peasants to transform into actors, like in Oberammergau? Or mobilize more cultivated villagers who, in any case, prefer smoking hashish or playing trictrac?

"Even the very name Osiris," they claimed, "is buried in Egypt. This god of the dead is too heavy a burden to carry."

But Layla didn't allow herself to get discouraged:

"The myth of Osiris," she pleaded, "is that of the eternal return of life. It can't die. You know very well that the name of Isis has remained popular. In the region around Hour, the hired women mourners imitate the magical gestures that Isis made in order to make Horus surge forth from Osiris's dead body and resurrect his corpse."

They told her to return to earth and give up on resuscitating the mysteries of ancient Egypt in an Islamic country, mysteries perpetuated in part by Christianity. Why not then the manger on the public square and Horus's four sons prefiguring the four evangelists of the Apocalypse! Wasn't Layla aware that no one wanted to live in the village with the flies, the viruses and the malaria any longer? She knew all that, but she loved her village, neighboring that of Hussein. She loved this earth of the Saïd where their roots were intertwined. She didn't hold it against her friends, but she saw very well that they were all living under Qaraqûsh's law.

The news that Layla was teaching at the university rapidly made its way through the Coptic community. She had a career, a salary.

"In today's world," said a woman in black, "that's better than owning stocks."

"The peasants no longer pay," added another woman. "After the big properties, the small ones will disappear. Work is a solid value."

Thus Layla became a value convertible into cash on the matrimonial market. Virtuous messengers came to see her mother. Madam Morcos powdered her nose, put on lipstick, hesitated between the navy blue dress brightened with a small white collar and the one she'd crocheted herself, the color of ancient gold, set off with gilt buttons; her children no longer permitted her to wear black except on days of mourning or for funerals.

"An alliance with your family would be an honor for us," said the messengers. "Our nephew is an officer; he's young, he has a future. Thirty pounds per month of private income, forty in pay. Your daughter is of a marrying age ..."

"Layla is almost thirty years old," they also slipped in. "If you wait too long, no one will want her; she'll remain 'fallow.' Our suitor is a professor, like her. They're made for each other. Don't let this chance go by."

"In today's world," answered Madam Morcos, "parents no longer marry off their children."

She did, however, make discreet inquiries before passing the messages to her daughter. She kept in mind only the irreproachable suitors.

Layla's relationships with intellectuals and artists, her frequent outings with Hussein, somehow didn't tarnish her reputation. Undoubtedly, the way she was treated as a professor henceforth protected her from the cackle of gossip.

"Morals have changed," people conceded. "Youth has to have its way. We can't send our girls to study abroad and forbid them from going out with young men. That won't prevent them from becoming excellent wives and good mothers."

And what was Madam Morcos waiting for? When Layla was sixteen, her mother had refused the idea of her premature burial in marriage. But Layla was almost thirty! Hussein? No, Madam Morcos's principles were far too rigid. Her daughter would never marry a Moslem. Yet she liked Hussein; if only he were a Copt! In truth, she didn't want to marry off her daughter, to separate herself from her and face solitude. After all, this friendship with Hussein was a shelter, a means of security, protection. Maybe Madam Morcos wasn't waiting for anyone.

Layla didn't give a damn about any of it. She and Hussein had been married since the beginning of time.

Their engagement was solemn. The setting was a temple ruin, and their witnesses were the sand and the sun. The young people embraced.

"We'll try to imitate the tender spouses of the Ancient Empire," said Hussein. "I'll plant a lotus in our garden and a cross of life on the threshold of our house. Together, we'll watch for the crescent moon in the sky; at harvest time, we'll gather the most beautiful sheaves of wheat and we'll fill large vases with them. There will be nothing but years of abundance for us. Others have already confronted society's anger, but anger has been worn out."

Layla laughed in order to hide her tears.

They wanted to build a big statue of a god, hollow like those in which the priests of Antiquity hid to pronounce the oracles. But they had only the sand and the wind. Hussein hid behind a mound; he spoke authoritatively:

"Cursed is he who turns woman away from the right path."

"The right path?" asked Layla in a very little voice. "I have no idea about that. Make a sign, just a little sign, so I'll know where to direct my steps."

The wind rose. The sand got into their eyes, their noses, their mouths; it covered their hair, their clothes. They were the color of sand, of desert. They were happy. No one else needed to know yet.

There was work for old women in black. The Copts among them were striving to marry Layla, the Moslems were taking care of Hussein. Hussein! An excellent match, he was often consulted at the Ministry of Planning; he had private interviews with the president.

The young Moslem women Hussein could have married were beautiful. One of them, descendant of a prominent Turkish family, wasn't afraid to belly dance in Cairo salons. Her long black hair stubbornly persisted in hiding white skin that some were dying to see, to caress.

"An abyss of beauty," some said.

"I'm not interested," said Hussein.

"A vision from paradise! Look at that belly turning and creating such dizziness leading to ecstasy!"

"I'm not interested," answered Hussein, "in the paradise of the Moslem mystic. I prefer the paradise made by the hand of man: socialism."

Another young woman was a descendant of the Prophet, nobility of nobilities. Of a Yemenite father, she had become passionate about the history of religions since she had begun to question hers. Her only sin was to be rich. Young people who have never been in need of anything have a solid prejudice against richness!

"They are born," people said, "to change the order of things, and they're going to start with their marriage."

Moustapha and Fakhr-el-Nissa loved each other in a rational manner. They lived happily in action, among colors and books; they also didn't feel the crazy desire to have a child. When one doesn't love madly, it's easy to hear the voice of reason: political militancy doesn't guarantee the security necessary for the life of a child.

Without being at the head of any particular political organization, Fakr-el-Nissa led them all. Her presence alone was an organizing principle, because of the enthusiasm radiating from her, because of the originality of her ideas, or simply thanks to her smile, which calmed tensions and mellowed bitterness. Her ambition? To mobilize all women for a specific project or for a distant goal; to attain power through numbers.

When she planted her easel in the fields, the peasant women pointed sympathetically at her.

"Here comes the *photographia!*" they said.

And they would pose with a lot of pride and a vague hope for immortality. Mobilize all of them? That was a generous vision.

Women had been granted political rights: the amended Constitution didn't specify that to be Egyptian depended on sex; on that point, the hard-fought battle had been promptly won. Why not spontaneously revive an indisputable past? From the beginning of Islam, as well as at the time of ancient Egypt's "paganism," women had enjoyed a status in no way inferior to that of men.

Fakhr-el-Nissa bustled about to create "temporary" societies dedicated to the political education of women. Temporary, it was agreed, in order to dodge possible legal harassment.

A long, difficult, tough battle was already on its way: that of the private status of women. It presented itself not as a battle between men and women, but as an assault, by the enlightened, on obscurantism. The cause of female emancipation was served at the time by the popular novels of Naguib Mahfouz who, in exploiting the taste of Egyptians for melodrama, made an entire people cry over the fate of the women of the lower middle class. A river of words unleashed a river of tears.

As for Layla, she discovered that she would have to free herself from the pompous seriousness associated with her doctorate. She didn't at all see herself learnedly exposing doctrines and dogmas. Demystify philosophy, measure the weight of religious precepts ... One could be learned without being serious; why not serious without being learned? Alas! Her degree required her to get along with official serious-mindedness, to wear its mask, although it might mean unmasking herself when she wanted to.

The number of students was growing. Taha Hussein[1] had insti-

---

[1] Taha Hussein: a renowned blind author who became minister of culture, democratized education and introduced the teaching of French in schools, so as to balance British influence.

tuted free education, thus renewing the renaissance begun by Mohamed Ali. And the Revolution was multiplying the number of schools; the university elite were covering administrative and teaching positions, welcoming children of the lower middle class, and hoping for more generations of peasants and workers to reach higher education. The new regime painted Doctor Morcos's career in glowing colors: he had been the son of a rich peasant; the poor peasant would also have his chance and this chance would be through the university. Thus the imagination flowed.

The least brilliant Baccalaureate students came to Layla's classes. The others entered schools thought to be nobler, and they attached little importance to philosophy. However, one had to have a university degree to become worthy of employment as a ledger clerk or state-approved employee ... or private. Exceptions to the rule existed everywhere: some students loved philosophy and Layla latched onto them. Or she stubbornly communicated the sacred fire to those elements that only chance had led into her classroom.

It must be said that she rarely succeeded, for the students had come to realize that the Bachelor's degree in philosophy didn't even open the way to the coveted jobs of clerks and scribners. A few years later the dignity of the state employee was automatically conferred to all Bachelor's degree students—thus opening the door to them all, at age twenty-two, to the security of an entire life of retirement!

Under these circumstances, Layla decided that dance was the most useful form of philosophy to teach; dance, in order not to suffocate under the weight of state-approved and private red tape ... dance, so as to forget the threat of unemployment.

One day she was given the responsibility of chaperoning a group of female students headed for Syria. She jumped with joy: she would again see mountains, forests, and countryside without dust!

On the boat, she spoke to the young women about dance, about Djalal-el-Din El-Roumi who founded the order of whirling dervishes and made of dance a prayer. And she realized how much these students were fascinated by those men who, in order to imitate the planets in their slow gravitational movement around an absolute center, God, whirled themselves around until they reached a state of complete exhaustion, loss of self, ecstasy.

"Whirling dervishes," she said, "taught us how to waltz, and we've forgotten their mysticism."

In her own fashion, she explained to them the reasons why the Pythagoreans had forbidden the consumption of broad beans:

"Broad beans swell up. They make you heavy. You can't dance easily if you eat too many of them."

And her students laughed. Was she going to tell them the story of her grandfather's second wife, buried in Hour under the broad beans? They already found her not very serious. After all, broad beans were the greatest source of protein for thin and gracious peasant women, because they didn't eat their fill.

But Layla liked to make the young women laugh.

The welcome they received in Syria was almost delirious. The tone was set by the brightly colored decorations at the port of Al Ladhiqiyah: Nasser's picture was everywhere. One beautiful sunny afternoon, after a long walk in the mountains, they gathered on a public square and danced the *dabka*, a Syrian farandole. Without fifes or tambourines, only their feet and hands gave rhythm to the dance. A guide, a handsome mountain man, happily led a line of Syrian peasants and Egyptian students. He improvised verses celebrating Arab nationalism and Nasser, his great inspirer. He sang for the liberation of the Palestinian people and for victory over Zionism. He denounced the love of Shamoun, the Lebanese, for the dollar, and of Dulles, the American, for oil. He prayed to birds and all that flies to carry messages of greeting to his beautiful Jamila and to Ben Bella in Algeria, and to carry curses to all the reactionaries of the Middle East. Thus the dabka went on, beating a thousand-year-old rhythm.

But an old professor, guardian of academic morality, scowled over the songs, the laughter and the farandole on the public square. He had Layla brought to him.

"You're giving a very bad example," he said, "you're showing your students the path of vice!"

A few students with long faces agreed.

"Righteous anger!" they cried out.

The trip ended in decency and boredom. Having studied in Paris, Layla, more than anyone else, was exposed to suspicions. She had to be twice as cautious. From contact with her friends, she had developed too much of a tendency to forget the fundamental laws of morality: respectability and secret doors. The old professor, steeped in piety, had opportunely reminded her of them.

One day, the old professor went to visit the *ghaouazi*, professional women dancers and conquerors of the heart. He'd left his sad face with his wife. A ghazia began to dance just for him. Her belly whirled and whirled and made him dizzy. He stood up, tied his belt around his waist and began to whirl his belly heavily, gaily. The ghazia took a cane, placed it between her legs; she danced slowly, looking into the eyes of the old professor, inexorably, so as to better see his excitement reach its height … She got paid the price of sensuality. At the height of his satisfaction, the old man spit on her, on all prostitutes, on all women whom a look can make into a prostitute. Ultimate and pathetic satisfaction!

Layla and Hussein liked to dance at the "Santa Lucia" in Alexandria because of Bob Azzam, who sang a pastiche of Alexandrian language, a savory mix of Arab, Italian, and French, to the rhythm of Westernized Oriental dances:
"Ya Moustapha, ya Moustapha
Wana Bahebak ya Moustapha …
… Chérie je t'aime, chérie je t'adore,
Come la salsa di pomodoro."[2]

They danced until late in the night. They felt at home. They ordered a dish of enormous shrimp for dinner. At the exit was an old dwarf who resembled Khamis or the god Bes, his long robe swelled by the sea winds, his arms full of jasmine necklaces.

"Bring us happiness, old uncle," they said to him.

"Give me what God has given you," chanted the dwarf. "He will give you even more."

Hussein bought a lot. He loaded Layla's neck with perfumed necklaces. The next day the flowers had faded, but the perfume lin-

---

[2] "Oh, Moustapha, Oh, Moustapha, …Darling, I love you, darling, I adore you, like tomato sauce."

gered with the image of a world of ancient gods.

On New Year's Eve, 1958, all those who had presented theses in Paris, London or Cambridge got together to bury the old year in the good Western tradition, with crackers and confetti, in a din of string and wind instruments. They wandered from dance hall to dance hall to prolong the illusion of joy that should spread over all the earth.

Between a stop in "Sahara City"[3] and another at "Mena House"[4] they waited at the foot of the sphinx for the sun to rise. They tried, in vain, to make a circle around a pyramid: with all of them together, they still could only reach around one corner. They waited for the first ray of sun in the crazy hope of capturing it. But the first ray was diffuse; they were unable to seize it. So they decided they would set up the stage of the sacred theater of Ancient Egypt there, in case the Kasr-Hour temple ruin wouldn't do.

"One day one of us will be the Minister of Culture. He'll have to remember."

At seven in the morning, the craziest among them decided to order their breakfast at the Mena House.

The police had also stayed up all night. They arrested Hussein and gave him just enough time to warn Layla.

Like a sleepwalker, Layla wandered in her car in search of her friends. She found Moustapha and Fakhr-el-Nissa at the Mena House. They had been expecting a wave of arrests since the Rayyis's speech the week before. Moustapha had his passport all ready and a visa for France: some students, ledger clerks, had ironed out the difficulties.

"Hide yourself carefully and don't worry," he said to Fakhr-el-Nissa. "I'll manage."

Near to Mena House, a bus was leaving for Alexandria at eight o'clock. Moustapha had the time to leave for France. The arrest warrant didn't arrive until after his departure.

Fakhr-el-Nissa took advantage of the political ignorance of certain members of her family to hide for a while, but fear ended up

---

[3] Sahara City: a nightclub, no longer in existence.
[4] Mena House: a luxurious colonial hotel opposite the pyramids.

reaching even the unconscious ones. She fled to the homes of fear-less friends who lived in the countryside; she disguised herself, she read a lot instead of painting. Alas! One of her hosts' cousins rec-ognized her and denounced her; he neither held a grudge nor did he have any scores to settle. He was simply afraid, the poor man, afraid to be suspected, to be contaminated, afraid out of habit; afraid of not knowing from where the accusation would burst forth that would send him in his turn to prison.

Fakhr-el-Nissa joined the women who were working at the Kanater-el-Khayreya dam: common law prisoners and political pris-oners mixed together.

The women dressed in black, who stitched tapestries or played bridge, those who enjoyed tea on sunny terraces or cared for their rheumatism in the beautiful hotels of Helwân, found a lovely sub-ject of conversation.

"That's what politics leads to. She wanted to do like the men! Well! Let her learn to live like men, in prison!"

The women whose sons, cousins or nephews Fakr-el-Nissa had refused in marriage, were delighted that they'd avoided that union.

Moustapha found temporary work in Paris; he attempted to alert the Western press. But who cared about Communists in Egypt?

Hussein rotted for a few months in Cairo prisons before being sent very far away to the oases of the western desert, to Khargah, where one cannot escape men without finding thirst and death.

Diffuse fear settled in. Not long before, when it was still a ques-tion of old deposed pashas, the majority laughed heartily:

"Ha, ha! He used to take on airs! See how he polishes his worn-out shoes so he can look dignified ... He's afraid of his former ser-vants. Why are they still leaving him his house?"

But other victims, enthusiastic young people with a future, also took their turn in the sad procession. Hussein, Fakhr-el-Nissa. A shiver of terror ran through the country and settled into hearts. Fear is an indispensable ingredient in the grand theater of politics.

As long as only the rich were affected by it, there had been hope that their money would serve the happiness of all. But the people found themselves empty-handed. With big words like "liberty" or "justice," they invented puns, which revealed a hint of bitterness. And they remained confident, happy, and full of hope drawn from the lightness of the air and the heat of the sun. They had two fathers: Allah in paradise, and on earth, Nasser.

Layla no longer knew what the word "traitor" meant. Who was a traitor? Her grandfather, who had believed it wiser to negotiate with the English, so as to be more quickly rid of them? Hussein, victim of an illusive game of seesaw between the Great Powers?

She was surrounded by men who were considered confident, though incompetent—perhaps especially incompetent! —who were holding important offices. The country was slowly breaking up.

Propaganda and indoctrination struggled in vain to "inflate a pierced goatskin." Popular spirit, cynical and lively, would put things back in their place:

"I was on the bus during rush hour. God sent me a guy who stood on my feet during the whole ride. I tolerated him as long as I could, then I said politely to him ... I was afraid, you know! I said to him: 'Is your Lordship an army officer?' He said no. 'So, son of a dog, get your feet off me!'"

The poor man had let himself be roughly handled, but he laughed. Indignation? That was the luxury of the well to do.

One by one, all those who did not want to live obscurely and mute under the dictator's spotlights, left. Living as refugees across the sea, they discovered an ardent nostalgia for their abandoned country. They accused exploitation and capitalism, development and underdevelopment. They studied how not to copy the defects and errors of the West. They gathered information about China and Cuba, hoping men would one day change, at home and elsewhere.

It was a slow and miserable exodus.

Layla remained alone. Her fate was not as sad as that of the wives of prisoners. In the street, when she ran into a cousin or an old friend, she didn't have to pretend to avoid him. The advantage of doubt: she wasn't Hussein's wife or even his fiancée. She was just an old maid.

She wanted to spread her indignation, her anger, like an earthquake, to chase away the vapors of fear, to de-mask abusive authority, destroy peace of mind and confidence in an all-powerful father. She was looking for weapons, words with dynamite. Kierkegaard had seen a threat to God and life itself in institutionalized authority. Nietzsche, who believed in the divine, had hoped for a new man, a chain of new men, creators and masters of the universe.

Feverish, Layla wrote Arabic words full of dynamite. She burned to communicate doubt and questioning to her students.

For two years she was passionate about Kierkegaard. She wrote a book, which was published. All of her students read it and congratulated her. They had exams to take, degrees to conquer ... The power of words didn't make walls crumble; Layla, skeptical and discouraged, continued to use them.

Her brother, Yehia, wore an eagle and three stars on his shoulder: he was a brigadier general. His friends from 1948 had taken power; he was content with the prestige conferred by a richly decorated uniform. His place in the family—that of the son who succeeds the loved and respected father—was ambiguous; his glory was awkward. He hid his malaise under a mask of cynicism, steel insensitivity. Left out of power and dispossessed of a part of their fortune, his elder uncles never missed a chance to reproach him. Impassive, he listened to them.

Nor did Layla stop throwing barbs at him. Yehia, who had always kept his private life from the family, didn't really understand why they quarreled with him about prisons.

"The Communists are traitors," he maintained with dignity. "They would hand over the country to Russia on a silver platter!"

"Well! It's been ages since you yourself sold us to the Russians!" stormed Layla.

The big brother laughed and patiently explained:

"No, we haven't been sold to the Russians. We're building our country with the help of all those who want to give us a hand."

Like a good soldier, he never let himself be rattled. Words that didn't fit with his opinion were no more than wind. When one wears an eagle and three stars on one's shoulder, one doesn't feel caught in a net like a quail.

"I'm not the one who makes politics," he said, when he ran out of arguments. "I'm a military man, I teach the art of war. I'm ready to make war when it's necessary."

Around this time, Yehia decided to get married.

The ceremony took place in the pretty little church of Zeitoun, near Heliopolis. As for the reception, it took place on the terrace of the Semiramis Hotel, overlooking the Nile. Small tables decorated with lanterns were set up for the dinner around two dance floors, one for the waltz and the twist, and the other for belly dancing. The important military men were there with their scintillating wives, so much like those of deposed pashas.

Madam Morcos discovered on this occasion that she had kept, much better than all the women of her entourage, her figure and her beauty. In her son's heart, did she still overshadow the new wife?

The celebration went on for a long time after dinner. In the distance, the pyramids, briefly pulled out of the dark by capricious moonlight, were swallowed once again by darkness. The desert extended beyond, encircling Hussein's prison ... They danced until morning, and for those who were too tired, Abd-el-Wahab came with his lute and sang languorous, melancholy love poems.

Ferdous, Layla's new sister-in-law, was gorgeous. She resembled the statue of Sesostris I, discovered in Licht: the same stature, the same rounded eyebrows above heavy eyelids, the same slightly disdainful fold on each side of her nostrils, contrasting with the general curve of sensuous lips.

The beauty of her daughter-in-law didn't impress Madam Morcos:

"She has the eyes of a big frog," she said.

Layla remarked that the frog was a divinity in Kasr-Hour, but her mother retorted that that had nothing to do with the aesthetics of eyes.

"Especially when they're accompanied by the lips of a Negress. As for her nose, wide and flat! I hate nothing so much as an ugly nose."

Against such unfounded prejudice, Layla quickly found herself out of arguments. She tried another approach:

"Her hair is smooth and wavy, she puts it up very elegantly. And her body? It has the shape of those statuettes used as make-up spoons in ancient Egypt."

Madam Morcos had to concede to those advantages, but she attacked again: "That name! Ferdous! A peasant name," which made her delicate nostrils tremble.

"Ferdous," cried Layla, "is the Coptic paradise. And the paradise of paradise for Moslems. Could one have a more beautiful name?"

Ferdous refused to share the Morcos paradise, claiming there was too much noise in Rodah.

Madam Morcos was disappointed. She'd planned on giving notice to the people renting the fifth floor of the house—an immense apartment with huge balconies—for the pittance of seven Egyptian pounds. She had hoped her son would one day take advantage of it, instead of paying six times as much for one of those tiny new lodgings with a low ceiling and poor-quality painting.

But Ferdous was feeding other ambitions. To house themselves, the men in high places had only the burden of choice: many properties had been dispossessed. It was just a matter of knowing the best strings to pull.

Yehia knew them. He prepared the different envelopes, each containing a certain number of Egyptian pounds, gave them to the right people and obtained a spacious apartment on the sixth floor of a house, set back slightly from the Nile, across from the Semiramis Hotel in a setting reminiscent of their wedding night.

Layla continued to sadly observe the evolution of her neighborhood: the old bourgeoisie was escaping to more serene and shaded areas, whereas the crowd of refugees from the canal, peasants who'd lost their lands, and small business owners, were infiltrating the neigh-borhood. Rodah had lost its romantic feel: the beautiful trees from times past seemed to have faded, worn out by the feverish agitation of the crowds. At dawn, the singing of the birds was lost in the commo-tion from the street, which didn't know how to sleep or wake up. The one-eyed street lamp disappeared one day to give way to eight huge electric lamps, floating like space ships flying above the busy streets ... like an attraction at an amusement park, but without the popular joy.

Stuck to the side of Ferdous's house was what they called, not without a sense of humor, "the other building." It was an assemblage of rooms one next to the other, built with walls of crude red brick, furnished with mats and bundles, each sheltering an entire family, often including the grandparents. A termite's nest of the disinher-ited who had again escaped the wrecker's pick. From Ferdous's bal-cony, Layla looked at this swarming with nostalgic hope, where all the silhouettes enveloped in large black sheets could have been poor Zebeida. She saw children playing with a ball made of rags sewn together, hens cackling in the center courtyard, women busy wash-ing laundry in water drawn from the public fountain. But no sign of Zebeida. The last time she'd seen her was on an evening of Ramadan. A little dried-out, shriveled creature, Zebeida had told Layla she'd return the next day at the hour of the *iftar*.[5]

Layla had waited, in vain, for a long time. The sunset had come, the cannon fired,[6] the call to prayer was chanted from the top of all the minarets. Lantern in hand, the children went from door to door begging for hazelnuts and small coins. But Zebeida didn't come.

Where was Zebeida?

Wahaoui, ya wahaoui ... With words that had no meaning, the little singers seemed to be saying that life and death made no sense either, and that joy or sadness could happen for no reason.[7]

---

[5] Iftar: during the month of Ramadan, Moslems neither eat nor drink from the rising of the sun until its setting. The iftar, meaning breakfast, is the meal taken after the sun sets. The sohour is the meal taken before the sun rises.

[6] The cannon fires in order to announce the beginning of the iftar.

[7] Wahaoui is a word that has no sense for modern Egyptians. But in ancient Egypt, it expressed an invocation to the moon.

Little by little, Layla became attached to Ferdous; the latter had been raised, like her, in a boarding school operated by nuns; she knew French, but beings and things interested her more than books.

Her sister-in-law's familiarity with fish fascinated Layla, as in the past had Zebeida's with the devil and the good Lord. Ferdous could have taught a thing or two to the people of Damiette themselves, reputed however to be great connoisseurs, for she maintained very friendly relations with the best fishermen in the country; those who fish deep sea mullet and salt it on board their huge-decked boats in order to sell it to the Saptiah merchants in Cairo; those who, torch in hand, venture to the beaches at night to surprise the lobsters. She had learned their secrets.

Ferdous could talk forever about the sharks and dolphins of the Red Sea. She initiated Layla into the joys of fishing and the life of the fisherman, over on the fine sand of the beaches of Hourghada. She was generous to a fault with her friends. The fishermen came and settled into her home in Cairo, sometimes to take out their young wives, sometimes to have their abscesses or their trachoma cared for in a clinic. Ferdous paid for their consultations with the family's doctors, to whom she served sumptuous meals. She even had the ambition of marrying Layla to one of those prosperous doctors.

Madam Morcos didn't at all appreciate this open door to anyone who came along.

"At the time of the Turks," she told Layla, "there were special houses to receive the dervishes who lived on public charity. At your brother's house, all they're missing are the dervishes. You become inhuman by dint of hospitality, and you end up doing nobody a favor."

In truth, Madam Morcos was worried about Yehia's finances. But Ferdous managed quite well. The grateful fishermen sent her fish. She was helped by maids whom she paid little, because she hired them in the village, "behind the gamousse," she said. She put herself to a lot of trouble teaching them to do their hair, to not skimp on the water they no longer had to carry on their heads, to bring out their rustic charm through a judicious choice of flowered dresses. Ferdous had a taste for peasant things, for peasant cooking too, with its weight in clarified butter. She sat in the middle of the kitchen, one maid on her right, one maid on her left—with Layla as the public—and with her voice directed the operations, the laughter and the verbal abuse.

The ancient Egyptians used the same ideogram, a human face, to express scorn and joy: Ferdous's face, maybe, in another life.

One day, Egypt went to war with Yemen. For the Revolution? For the Empire?

Ferdous was subconsciously delighted to see Yehia leave, for war, they say, is a source of income, and when one wears an eagle and three stars on one's shoulder, one can hope to earn a lot of money.

Yehia left for the war with the hope of putting into practice what he'd been teaching. He came back from it sickened. No, war was not the art he'd imagined. War was a dirty job, and the Egyptians weren't made for it. Why would a people, to whom despair is foreign, make war?

Out of necessity, Yehia continued his career. But he was already a different man, profoundly disillusioned. He saw bitterly the number of Copts decrease in the corridors of power.

"It's the logic of change and the revolution you defended so much," observed Layla. "The ruling class had to be renewed."

But Yehia had no taste for this change. For him, the Moslems remained the people who had betrayed the religion of their ancestors. Layla could very well tell him this ancestral religion contained in it all the past and present avatars of monotheism. A military smile, full of disdain for literary hacks, formed on his lips. Strong with the feeling of the superiority of the Copts, he let Layla utter her nonsense.

If only they would give him a position of power in the army! But power wasn't given to competent people. Never in his lifetime would he avenge the humiliation of 1948. He knew the army was made for parades, amusement, and especially for maintaining order.

His position guaranteed him beautiful houses on the Red Sea and the former royal pavilion of Hourghadah. He often went there with Ferdous to enjoy fishing for shark and to give himself the illusion of war.

From the coast, one often sees dolphins going by, one eye open at the surface of the water. Sharks don't dare attack them. Because of the color of their skin? No, on that score, Yehia knew more than Ferdous.

"Dolphins know how to fight," he explained. "When one of their little ones has just been born, all of the adults surround the mother and child in order to protect them against the sharks who come running at the odor of the blood of childbirth!"

Alas, dolphins did not inhabit Egypt.

Hussein was still in prison.

Family and tradition had closed again around Layla. She was told that she was no longer a child, that she had to defend the rights of the Coptic community. But Layla was not stirred by the call. Beyond this whole family whom she loved, beings like her uncles whom she respected, there were Copts who had found shrouds in tombs on earth freshly shifted by the Nile, and who had cut them up into pieces to share the booty; priceless Coptic shrouds! And then there were the monks who seemed to have been born old and doomed to laziness, and who had only renounced women, creatures of the devil, because they preferred young boys. And the cloistered nuns of the subterranean neighborhood of old Cairo who live in long dark corridors, beneath a mass of robes they rarely dare take off for a bath! Egypt, cradle of monachism, land of saintliness? But the names of Anthony, Bakhoum, and Macaire reminded her only of a tradition that forbids laughter, the work of the devil, as is woman. No, Layla was not ready to get excited for the cause of the Coptic community.

She desired nothing so much as to marry Hussein. She feared above all the dictates, the edicts and what was forbidden by fanaticism.

Defend the religion of the Copts? Layla preferred the prefigurations of Christianity drawn on the walls of the Pharaoh's temples and the mystery of the Trinity which includes the love of women and the strength of animals. Why had Christianity made the Trinity the business of men? It smelled of vice.

In Kom Ombo, the father god, Sobek, has a crocodile head, the son god, Penebtaoui, is a young child, and the mother goddess,

Hathor, sometimes a woman, sometimes a cow, is a goddess made wholly of grace and joy, a principle of love between the father and son. The father crocodile bursts from the depths and symbolizes rebirth, eternal life, and the eternal return of life. He gets old, he dies, he lives, renewed, through his young child.

On the walls of the temple of Denderah, the god's son is a musician like his mother Hathor. He carries a sistrum in his hand and is called Ihy. A cheerful god and a music lover made to pass through like a musical note and return with other notes.

The beautiful images of the Trinity on the walls of temples did not create fanaticism. Between that Trinity and the unique god of Islam, there were no Crusades.

Layla liked the pagan legend of Jesus Christ that makes of him an initiated magician in Egyptian sanctuaries. Perhaps similar to one of those monks of El-Moharrak, with the eyes of a clairvoyant, on the soil of Hermopolis, where Christ supposedly celebrated the first mass in the presence of his disciples. Ah! If Egypt were ever sacred ground, if those monks still had magical power, they needed to make one miracle: sweep away fanaticism. But they were just poor monks. Those who preceded them in the desert maybe saw Amon, the hidden one. But they ...

The Christianity of the Copts is too much like all other religions. The Coptic language? But those hieroglyphics spelled out in Greek reminded Layla of another colonization. She remained puzzled, however, at the memory of a foreigner who breathed sound into the pictograms of the Rosetta stone. Some Copts, refugees in Paris after the campaign of Egypt, had given him the means to do so. From 1801 on, they gathered in Pavé Street, around Don Rafaël. They taught Coptic to Champollion, and the scholar began speaking Coptic all alone, out loud, translating in Coptic everything that went through his head, dreaming in Coptic and in Egyptian ...

Layla knew Coptic was necessary to decipher the hieroglyphs, but she would like it to have been strangers or Egyptians converted to Islam who would take over their study. "Culture has no borders," she thought. "I don't need to pay this tribute to fanaticism. So what were those Copts going to do in Paris if they hadn't collaborated

with Bonaparte? It was the epoch of the Mamelouks. More foreigners! Strangers against strangers! Those millennia of occupation
… Nasser was the first Copt, in a millennium, to rule the country.
Converted to Islam, but a Copt all the same, like eighty percent of
the population. The foreigner swore to bring about his downfall,
and he put some people in prison and gave others the bright spectacle of a tyrant's court. And now Copts wanted to give value to
their rights against Moslems. When the boat was on the verge of
sinking?"

In order to console herself about so many absurdities, Layla
began to draw hieroglyphs: lips to write that little word, *vers*,[8] lips
that made her want to kiss everything, gave her the illusion of loving
everything in spite of absurdity; and the oxhyrinchus,[9] forked fish
bodies, sharpened as if for bursting an abscess: they're used to writing the name of the god Bes, the dwarf so beautiful in his ugliness,
with his immense phallus whipping the universe, to provoke its
laughter and wake it up from its intolerable seriousness. The image
and the idea based on the image.

Layla lost the sense of time. She liked hieroglyphs, but not out
of ancestral pride: when one is born a mosquito of giant ancestors,
one has every interest in leaving the ancestors to all of humanity,
like the obelisk on the Place de La Concorde. She was simply
delighted that she could still write, awkwardly, like them.

A still-living civilization was perishing before her eyes, and she
was being asked to bring another one back to life. Already, the wandering poet who sings the adventures of Abu Zeid, Khalifah and
Diab could no longer be heard: no one any longer knew the epic of
Beni Helal or the verses of Zanati. Hardly did a poet still come to sing
his ballad, accompanied by a rebab, on the stage of Sahara City.
Layla's students manipulated the Arabic language poorly. The beautiful voice of the muezzin, falling from the minaret, was projected
through a booming loudspeaker. To be heard, the sacred word needed
a gadget.

---

[8] Vers: toward.

[9] Oxhyrinchus: the fish who devoured Osiris's phallus, and who represents rebirth.

CHAPTER 8

Osiris's Resurrection

Hussein, Fakhr-el-Nissa and six hundred other Communists spent five years in prison. One spring day in 1964, on the eve of a visit by Khrushchev to Cairo, they were liberated. The Russian and the Egyptian had felt the need to smile at each other.

Hussein took more time arriving from the depths of the desert than did his sister. Another man, another woman. A few wrinkles. White hair at their temples. Lips pinched from holding back the flood of revolt for five years.

A lot of friends were missing from the group. Moustapha? From Paris, he had gone to Algiers where he'd found a position in the new university. He'd arrived full of enthusiasm for this country that had won its revolution. Two months, three months. He hadn't been paid. An administrative delay? ... Five months, six months; his savings were vanishing. He had news of Fakhr-el-Nissa only from the newspapers or from friends traveling abroad. From time to time a letter reached him. Censored. Never any answers to his questions.

One day he'd taken his life. A razor slash on the correct artery. One drowns quickly in one's own blood; what's important is not to miss. A child spoiled by life, he'd no longer been able to tolerate misery and unhappiness.

Hussein and Fakhr-el-Nissa rediscovered an Egypt whose face had changed. The Cooperatives coordinated the means of cultivation and production; fields overflowed into the desert; a large fertile valley was drawn between Cairo and Alexandria. The land planted with sugar cane had doubled. Corn had multiplied out of control.

Delicate, fresh, velvety vegetables had tripled in quantity. In Layla's neighborhood, incense was sometimes burned over the merchant cart, to protect the vegetables from the evil eye.

The population, too, was overflowing: between the census of 1882 and that of 1966, it had increased almost fivefold.

The old man, everywhere the same, hid behind the pious appearance of fasting and prayer, all the while watching over the proper functioning of corruption. The old man was becoming democratized and was multiplying. They said he could squelch every revolution from its outset.

Fakhr-el-Nissa had had as much as she could take of politics. She'd seen too many women in prison who had slept next to her, below, above her. For five years, she'd smelled their odor, seen their tears and their faces without make-up made heavy by boredom and sleep, heard their cries, their secrets. Never tiring, she had kept painting them, always covered with a large veil so as to show only the face, its questioning, its anguish, its desire for liberty, and hands made of bones and misery, gripping prison bars.

She was obsessed with prison bars. Everywhere that five women were gathered together, she smelled the odor of prisons. In the past, she had struggled for the cause of political rights. What for? At each election the number came in, which had become mythical: 99.9% of voices in favor of Nasser ...

Dedicated, however, to reproducing the image of woman, Fakhr-el-Nissa continued to walk around with her easel and palette, but she needed, henceforth, the bright colors of the sun: orange, red, yellow, green, and blue. Grayness belonged to another epoch, to forgetting, to what was secret.

However, one time she renewed her ties with militancy.

Her cousin Fatma, a friend during good and bad days, had received a thirty-five year old husband from her family for her seventeenth birthday. A handsome man, infatuated with himself, he had offered her, on their wedding night, all of the love letters written to him by other women. In order to teach her a bit about life, he had explained that he hadn't married out of love, a fantasy of ignorant women her age, but only to guarantee his family an heir; her goal in life could only be to give him a son similar to himself. Every evening, he left the house to go play trictrac and laugh with his friends. Fatma prepared him nice little dishes in order to keep him home. A waste of time. She had a child. Misfortune! It was a girl.

Her spouse became doubly vulgar. Disgusted, Fatma asked for a divorce. The trial dragged on for years. The child grew up; she was seven, then nine and the trial still dragged on. Her husband had the right to claim the child; he demanded his little girl and at the same time the return of his wife to their home. Didn't the Prophet command that he could enjoy his wife?

The judgment was going to be handed down. Since the divorce had never been pronounced, Fatma would be required to return to the marital home she detested.

That's when Fakhr-el-Nissa and her rediscovered friends decided to go en masse to the trial, dressed in clothing made of loudly rustling material.

A prison guard recognized Fakhr-el-Nissa and warmly shook her hand. An old friendship! Fatma's friends settled into tight rows in the balcony of the courtroom. Each time they stood or sat down, they demonstrated their haunting presence. When the judge opened his mouth to pronounce the sentence, they all got up in one movement and the noise of the faille and taffeta combined electrified the audience. Standing silently, they seemed to incarnate celestial justice.

The judge, impressed, handed down a sentence opposite of what everyone expected: Fatma was not at all required to return to her home.

Outraged, the prison guard pointed at Fakhr-el-Nissa:

"I recognize her! She's an agitator. Five years in prison weren't enough for her!"

"Religious laws can't be changed," the doctors had proclaimed.

Too bad! They would make morals change. Little by little, the laws would become obsolete and be nothing more than witnesses of the past.

Fakhr-el-Nissa drew the portrait of her cousin, Fatma, and hung it in the place of honor in her studio, where the sun strikes at full noon. But her militant activities stopped there.

Layla didn't want Hussein to be involved in politics anymore. She herself had avoided it, in spite of those who denounced her "negativistic" attitude.

"It's a nest of vipers," she repeated to Hussein.

"But," argued Hussein, "if honorable people pull out of politics, they leave it to the crooks!"

One year after the prisons were opened, the Communist Party decided to dissolve itself and to join with the only party, the Arabic Socialist Union.

"How can you do politics with a single party?" asked Fakhr-el-Nissa.

"By coloring it," answered Hussein. "Nasser is enough for our people. There isn't room for a battle among parties and the illusion of democracy."

Russia weighed the situation, but it wasn't at Egypt's door, and one could hope to use Russia without being used by her. Age progressively pulled Hussein away from Marxist abstractions. He understood that the sacrosanct vocabulary didn't apply to the Egyptian people, respectful of hierarchies, little inclined toward overcoming itself, always ready to smother by its fantasy the seriousness of the theory. Above the heads of the masses, the class war was unfolding within a thin layer of the privileged of society. Reforms would owe very little to theories imported from the West.

In spite of the power of Russia, the communist ideal remained; in spite of all, a hope in this Near East that had to be renewed without recourse to religious fanaticism.

Layla and Hussein were going to be married; henceforth, they announced it publicly.

In Hussein's family, they pretended to be offended. They looked very curiously at the foreigner who was doubly foreign, and Madam Zaghloul, a long-time friend, veiled her tender look with suspicion.

From Layla's side of the family, the reaction was even more violent.

"You have dishonored the family!" cried out the youngest of her aunts.

Her younger brother wrote her a severe letter beginning with these words: "I wouldn't have believed you capable of doing that." As for Yehia, he burst out with disdain:

"I thought you had principles."

Madam Morcos said she was "stabbed in the back" and took to her bed for several days. Only the elderly uncle showed indulgence: he was expecting something new from Layla and Hussein.

Having been united for so long by laughter, Layla and Hussein decided to make fun of public opinion. They married quietly. Hussein chose a gold wedding ring set with turquoise stones, representing a cobra, for Layla. Formerly, the goddess Isis made a similar cobra with silt, to bite the god Râ and tear his secret name from him, this magical name, thanks to which she would return life to the dead body of Osiris. A popular piece of jewelry: the cobra to chase away evil, turquoise to keep the evil eye far away, a spiral to prevent the circle from closing.

Fakhr-el-Nissa secretly made masks: heads of phoenixes, cows, vultures, donkeys, ibises, monkeys, frogs.

"With human bodies," she said, "we'll have a Sphinx theater. We'll be able to play the Resurrection of Osiris in the Temple of the Frog. The actors must be sphinxes capable of metamorphosing, for in ancient Egypt, the god Râ is embodied in different forms and his hidden name is not knowable. Only Isis knew it, but she kept the secret. Nor did she tell us what is written in the book of Thot. But each day, Râ is born, transfigured."

Layla and Hussein each earned fifty Egyptian pounds. With extra hours, correcting exams and the sale of their books to a student clientele, they were just barely able to gather between the two of them one hundred Egyptian pounds per month; enough to live in modest comfort. The revenues from their land, which had permitted them to pursue brilliant studies abroad, now counted near to nothing in their budget. They no longer took the trouble to go to the village in order to do the books with the peasants. They left the care of running the business to the scribes and the bursars. Nationalized stocks and bonds were worth their weight in paper, and the rent from the house evaporated in expenses and taxes. Madam Morcos and Madam Zaghloul regularly nibbled on their capital so they could offer themselves the little luxuries to which they'd become accustomed. They made a great effort not to depend financially on their children.

In order to save money, Layla and Hussein decided to live in the Rodah house. Madam Morcos evicted the people on the fourth floor so she could move in securely, be above the crowds and at the same time liberate her large apartment for the young couple.

A butcher opened his shop in front of the main bedroom window. Enormous, majestic, he sharpened his knife, and with his thumb moistened by saliva, he slid it nimbly along the blade, looking for a possible nick on the edge. Traveling restaurants were appearing with their little vehicles decorated like the cupolas of the palaces in *The Thousand and One Nights*, on the sides of which one could read: "Allah is with pious men who fear him," or "Allah loves those who suffer hardships with patience."

"Such good Christians, those Moslems!" said Hussein ironically.

Then one day he prophesied:

"One day, however, they won't allow themselves to be stepped on any longer."

Fakhr-el-Nissa often came and settled onto Layla's large veranda in order to paint the women who stocked up at these traveling kitchens. She had lost the reformist ardor of her youth. She painted the words of the Koran with all of the tenderness she felt for the common people.

"After all," she murmured, "abandonment to God helps them live. What will become of all these women when this trust is taken away from them?"

The years in prison and the death of Moustapha had emptied her inside. She strolled about in order to capture an image. Would she find the staircase where Moses had been saved from the waters?

From among the old furniture of the house, Layla and Hussein kept only the large copper brazier in the form of an Egyptian minaret. All winter, it looked at them with its blazing charcoal eyes. On the big walls, there was henceforth room for the tapestries of the illiterate children of Wissa Wassef and for the paintings by Egyptian artists in search of the people's soul: circles of pigeons, groups of donkeys, horses dancing, Nubians or peasant women from El-Saïd with ochre skin and tawny veils. Lamps made of a plaster stand encrusted with pieces of brightly colored glass replaced the old chandeliers made of Bohemian crystal; stained wood replaced the oak doors and permitted the north wind to blow through the apartment during the summer. The old hands of Fatma discovered in junk shops were substituted for bronze handles; a large reproduction of Isis carrying Horus's child helped them to forget the virgin embroidered in point passe by Madam Morcos, and Layla's portrait, painted by Fakhr-el-Nissa, replaced that of Doctor Morcos.

Hussein dug a pond in the garden; he planted lotuses—similar to those from which gods from India and China had surged forth, as in Egypt—and also papyrus.

Once public opinion got used to their marriage, right-thinking people came to visit the young couple. They found neither a Chippendale dining room, nor a Louis XVI bedroom! A scandalous rumor went around the city.

"Straw baskets, trays made of palm fronds! They got their furniture at the homes of peasants from El-Saïd and the bakers of the poor neighborhoods! Hussein explained to me that those are objects dating from ancient Egypt and they're called as they used to be in the olden days: *offa, ma'taf, meshanna.* I told him what I thought of their peasant taste!"

"Did they show you the Turkish coffee pots displayed in the hallway?"

"They have an incense burner in their living room. It appears to be for burning incense over guests who are sacred."

"They didn't burn incense over me. What about you?"

"Their house is a real junk shop!"

Yes, a real junk shop in the image of their culture. They had hoped to discover an element of eternity in the relics of innumerable civilizations: a brightly colored vase among porcelain debris, mixed in with the ruins of an ancient temple; a text engraved on the worn-out face of a millstone. But they arrived too late.

Everything found in beautiful Egypt has been enclosed in museums. The rest has disappeared, decomposed like palace bricks and houses of old, from which there remains only dust, still used as fertilizer.

New acquaintances went abroad and joined old friends. The war of Yemen continued, exuding scandal.

"Leave. Leave before the shipwreck," said their friends, happy, however, at the bottom of their hearts, to see them stay.

"We're not abandoning a sinking boat," they answered proudly.

"I'll never be able to paint anywhere else than in Egypt," added Fakhr-el-Nissa.

Their life followed its course.

One day, the Rayyis decided to try a grand coup, provoke a distraction and pull out of Yemen. To run and help the Syrians being harassed by the Israelis. Threaten the latter with closing their access to the port of Akaba. Demand—just for the sake of form?—the withdrawal of the United Nations peacekeeping forces.

The whole Arab world applauded loudly. In Cairo salons, people rubbed their hands together with satisfaction. Servants gathered around the grocer's radio, fellahs sat glued to the village café radios; suddenly everyone was talking about the master's coup.

"Nasser is strong. He set a real trap for them! Let's hope the Israelis don't escape him this time!"

The trick was well played. For the audience, the armies of the United Arab Republic paraded in the streets of Cairo; this proud

Goliath ready to smash little David created enthusiasm. Can a
Burmese understand the mentality of a Saïdy? U Thant, then General
Secretary of the United Nations, ordered the peace-keeping forces
to withdraw. There was no longer anything to come between the
Israelis and the Egyptians.

"We're going to throw the Israelis into the sea!"

In the streets of Cairo, the thundering loudspeakers took up
the phrase, accompanied by a chant by Om Kalsoum, which the
people found more to their taste than military marches. But the
whole West, impervious to the subtleties of the Egyptian verb, began
trembling for the Israelis.

Arabic children living abroad were advised not to go to school
in order to escape public anger; the anger of those who had kept
quiet under Nazism, in the face of concentration camps, in the face
of the crematoria; the anger inherited from parents who had closed
the doors of their country to Jews threatened with total extermi-
nation. A phenomenon of projection? Psychoanalysis gives a lovely
name to hypocrisy. If the Arabs represented such a danger, why then
had the Jews been encouraged to settle in the heart of an ocean of
hatred?

Layla had painfully picked herself up from the trauma of 1956,
which had made her want to destroy in herself all French culture, all
ties with the West. And now, from the other side of the sea, friends
with whom she had reconciled were trying to kill the Egyptian in her,
guilty of wanting to throw the Jews into the sea. The phenomenon of
projection was aimed at her. Why was she being accused of wanting
to massacre the Jews? For thousands of years, her people had lost the
power of massacring anyone, and the military parade could trick only
superficial observers. For thousands of years, her people had been
sleeping. The Egyptians were kept from waking because they didn't
know how to make war, like the dolphins of the Red Sea.

She had never known how to detest the Jews. She pitied them;
this West, of which they were culturally and economically a part,
rejected them. The ghetto followed them everywhere. They carried
in them the ghetto, because they were different from others. A
chosen people, perhaps, but hated as a chosen people can be.

Sometimes masters, here and there; at home, nowhere.

She measured the West's hatred for the Jew against the aggressiveness it showed toward her, the Egyptian who wanted "to throw the Jews into the sea."

A people elected by God came and imposed themselves on a people who incessantly recited the word of Allah and that of Nasser; the world exploded in a gigantic noise of arms. The tumult lasted only six days; Allah's adorers were too busy laughing. On the first morning, while the big men in the army were still feasting, the Israelis nailed the Egyptian air force to the ground. Without aerial cover, the Egyptians died of thirst in the Sinai. The defenseless Palestinians left the new occupied territories and went to swell the camps with refugees. With the voice of a bully, we had cried out to the chosen people of God "we will throw you into the sea!" and the chosen people of God, coldly busy making history rather than laughing, were silently throwing into the sea—into the sea or into the desert, it didn't matter—another people. The Arab children living abroad could return to school and be subjected to the mocking laughter of their classmates.

"Take off your shoes so you can run faster!"

Layla and Hussein desperately tried not to hurt one another. For Hussein, the Moslem, believed himself to be doubly humiliated because of Layla's look, that of a Copt, which weighed like a judgment, like the condemnation of an entire civilization to which he belonged. Yet Layla was tied to the common fate. Islam, fraternal link between a Russian, a Mauritanian, an Egyptian, could it separate an Egyptian from another Egyptian? What a strange thing is man, who only seeks out his brother so as to better separate himself from his brother!

A trip to Europe, the first since 1956, aggravated their wound and yet brought them closer. Some of their friends didn't want to see them. Others explained very delicately to them that they were gaining nothing by placing themselves under the banner of the Russians.

Only a few understood their profound wound and sympathized with them.

And the unknown passersby who made contact with them through a bit of conversation looked at them, surprised:

"Are you really Egyptians?" they asked, seeming to say: "You're not so stupid after all!"

Layla and Hussein had no contact with banks, but they read the press, and their contacts with publishing houses allowed them to measure Jewish power.

The West became hostile to them. Only de Gaulle, who was fighting Nazism and the crematoria, remained a friend. But he didn't reflect the feelings of all the French.

More than ever, they became enemies of themselves; but they did so together.

In despair, the people waited. The Rayyis had one day said his mea culpa, and the entire people, the good people of Egypt, had said to him: "You are our father. Everyone makes mistakes. We have confidence in you. You'll bring us out of this impasse. You're the only man in all of Egypt who can save us!"

Hussein believed in Nasser's genius. Madam Morcos, who loved the Rayyis, prayed day and night, and Sunday at church, so that God would make him victorious.

"God," she said, "punishes the strong when he crushes the weak. You'll think of me when I'm dead."

The people of Egypt also prayed for victory, morning and night, Friday at the mosque and Sunday at church. But on Saturday, at the synagogue, other peoples were praying for the Arab to be finally crushed.

Two children were born to Yehia and Ferdous. The first was named Matouschaleh, because an old aunt had dreamed he would live as long as the biblical Methuselah. The second was named Menkarios, because Yehia hoped to have fathered a pyramid builder.

Layla and Hussein blamed their difficulty in living with defeat on a house empty of children. Layla resorted to medical care. She finally became pregnant and greatly rejoiced. Hussein surrounded Layla with innumerable forms of attention: he watched her weight, her meals. Madam Morcos constantly gave advice to her daughter. She told her about all of her pregnancies, sparing her no details of her rapid and easy deliveries.

Madam Morcos was already rejoicing in being a grandmother for the third time when she unconsciously sacrificed her life, or what remained of it, in order to save that of little Menkarios. One day, while having fun watching the passersby out of the window of the fifth floor, he leaned over too far, teetered and fell. Instinctively, Madam Morcos rushed to catch him ... Heavier than he was, she arrived first on the sidewalk and absorbed the shock of the child's fall. He came out with a broken leg and a few bruises. Madam Morcos didn't have the time to suffer. The shock had killed her immediately.

They wept a lot for her; they envied her just as much for having known how to save her life from old age.

One misfortune, it is said, never comes alone. Layla's child was stillborn. All the powers of medicine could not give her another. So she did what Gamila had done. She remembered all of Zebeida's recipes. She visited all the tombs, around which, perhaps, souls floated. Birds, similar to the doubles of ancient Egyptians, inhabited her imagination. All she would have to do was tame her child who'd become a bird! Thot and Isis had the secret.

She persistently decoded the words on the walls of the tombs meant to restore life to the souls of the dead. She became passionate about the myth of Osiris, dead and resurrected, and the peasant customs that perpetuated the myth.

Osiris's sweat, derived from Elephantine, was in all the waters made sacred by the recitation of magic words. Ah! If only her child had been bathed in those sacred waters like the peasants do! If she had kept the umbilical cord of her child! Maybe she should have buried it like Horus buried that of Osiris, like the peasants still bury that of their son under the threshold of their house, so that the child will be reborn. In times past there existed a priest of the royal placenta.

But Layla had passed through the Enlightenment. One must pardon a mother for having believed in the double of her son, for having cried with this dead son over the umbilical cord devoured by a toilet flush.

"She's going crazy," said the mother-in-law. "An old maid always stays an old maid, even after marriage. My poor Hussein won't have a child."

Layla bitterly reminded her that Hussein was older than her by five long years.

"A man," said the mother-in-law out loud, "never ages."

And quietly, as if to herself:

"What an idea to go and marry an old maid!"

Hussein refused to adopt a child. What for? Before God and men, by virtue of Moslem law, this son would carry the name of his real father. They would get used to an empty household. Layla would begin to write books again. "Books are like children." To console himself, Hussein played the reed pipe. He peopled his desert with melancholy notes.

Despair spread slowly, stealthily, around them. They found themselves crushed in the mill of the Cold War. They despaired of liberating the country from two occupations: that of the Israeli enemies and that of the Russian friends. The war budget erased all prospects of a better life. Corruption became democratized, went from the ruling spheres to the inferior rungs of society. People moaned a lot; people fasted just as much, with all the force of despair, which would perhaps cause the unexpected to burst forth, from the bottom of the abyss.

The Copts had always fasted copiously during Lent and Advent, with the fifteen supplementary days that permit God to authorize marriages between cousins. They fasted because they'd made a wish, or because they liked the food served on fasting days, or because these good dishes didn't cost very much. They cooked with oil. They sometimes substituted water for oil out of a spirit of asceticism or out of care to avoid serious stomach acid.

The Moslems also fasted: all during the Ramadan moon, from

sunrise to sundown, they neither drank, nor ate, nor smoked. Layla's and Hussein's servant fasted, furthermore, during the moon of Ragab, in order to be pardoned for a false oath. In the evening, he participated in the Zikr led by the dervishes around the walls of the mosque. With others, he became drunk in the name of Allah. "Allah! Allah! Allah!" he chanted, mixed in with the powerful choir of pious men, with a rhythmic movement of the entire body, forward, backward, to the side, to a crazier and crazier rhythm. The angels surrounded him, and up there in the sky, Allah repeated his name, like he repeated the name of Allah, in states of trance and ecstasy. And his false oath had no more importance at all.

They fasted for a number of days, over the most obvious part of the year. They had prayer orgies. They constructed mosques and churches next to mosques. The Minister of the legacy of Mortemain, charged with spreading Islam, could dispose of great fortunes, and the Church of Saint Mark did its best to not let itself be outdone. Beautiful building materials were used for these houses of God. And fountains to purify the faithful or to provide for holy water. They didn't think about those who led the prayers. But the loudspeakers made sure that Christ and Allah or Allah and Christ heard the voices of men!

The houses of poor peasants were built of dry earth, ready to return to dust as soon as they made contact with water ...

They paraded in prayer. Processions crossed each other in the streets of the city: Parades of Copts, parades of Moslems. Later, one day when fatality was at its most profound, sparks flew; the stronger massacred the weaker. It was in Choubrah El-Kheima. A day of insanity. This little bit of earth, saturated with dust, smothered under asphalt and countless numbers of shoes, dirtied by the smoke of factories, this little bit of earth had the chance to no longer inhale the widespread bloodshed. But an entire people cried about it and cursed despair.

An ingratiating atmosphere of defeatism settled in. It was known, since the Six Day War, that the Egyptian people were not made for war. Israel was a fait accompli. All attempts to smash it ended in loss. This time, the Palestinians were not the only ones to pay the price; Egypt had sacrificed its territorial integrity. The canal remained closed, the Sinai occupied. Israel! They had to learn to live with it as with a cancer or an artificial transplant, a biologically foreign body.

Israel, which was pushing the Palestinians far away, in order to survive, was also fighting against a cancer: that of poverty and of numbers, capable of making everything explode. Absurd destiny. Tragedy.

Layla refused despair and defeatism. The Rogers plan reflected the hope of a negotiated peace. Everywhere in Egypt, people believed they saw a great light. Why not? Wasn't there an ancient tradition in Egypt that nothing was impossible?

The Minister of Public Health gave proof of this that summer when cholera threatened. A competent team took the situation in hand, sending out big vehicles loaded with insecticides, reinforced with aerial support. Regiments of sweepers cleared the streets of all the national garbage. Radio and television were called upon to indoctrinate the people. People were witness to a veritable mass uprising against figs and grapes, flies and mosquitoes. Their armies were smashed.

"Everything is possible in Egypt," said Layla stubbornly. "Look on the temple walls at men becoming living Osirises."

Fakhr-el-Nissa didn't contradict her; yes, everything would be possible if they could mobilize the women. But she no longer wanted to. The doctors who bought her paintings, and courted her a bit, told her it was essential to liberate women from the authority of men, to give them work outside the home and thus control the birth rate. Fakhr-el-Nissa pinched her lips together:

"That will be for someone other than me. I'm tired. I want to live and not despair any further."

Hussein, an ardent defender of official power, was officially optimistic. He insisted on the progress made by Egypt, in spite of herself: education for everyone, equal chances for all; peasant and worker social structures, burst forth from nothing; communal life created by the cooperatives; the slow but sure industrialization of the country. As for the war against Israel, "we have to count on time, which will be in favor of the Arab countries."

What he didn't say was that the weight of disappointed hopes, of accumulated despair, frightened him; as did the misery of the landless peasant in his house of dried silt, which a water leak could destroy.

At the end of the summer in 1970, hijackings were headline news. The well-to-do of the world became frightened of this vague, blind threat that scorned the protective laws of the earth's privileged. But among the desperate were many who laughed at the spectacle of the rich caught in a trap. All of the stored-up hatred of the slums was liberated.

Then the laughter froze. For the powerful, too many interests were at play. The screws had to be turned. The show had to be stopped at any cost. In bygone days, in the time of myth, Seth killed his brother Osiris and cut him into pieces in order to deprive him of eternal life. Then Cain killed Abel. The brother always killed the brother. And the Jordanian Arab killed the Palestinian Arab. A fiction separated them: the name of a state, instituted by the British, dating only from the recent past. The Arab, whose interests were threatened, killed the poor brother who threatened his interests. The indestructible myth weighed heavily, and the eternal game reached supreme refinement—make one believe in the meanness of the one being killed, or in his goodness, according to the country to which one belongs. And order, an unstable order, was re-established.

The press didn't talk at all about Hussein's, Layla's, Fakhr-el-Nissa's and all their friends' nausea. States want nothing to do with outdated sentimentality. Empire builders scorn weak dispositions.

Layla took her daily ration of the absurd; as soon as the sun came up she listened to the news. Politics didn't allow her to live, and nothing, not even a child, could cure her of this great nausea she experienced upon awakening.

Hussein! His name means strong, virtuous, difficult to reach. Would he go to the dogs like the others, like everyone else?

Fawzia Assaad

One day the Rayyis of Egypt died. He died, like Doctor Morcos, of a heart attack.

The Egyptians lost a father. But Egypt didn't remain a widow like Madam Morcos. She cried hysterically the first day, less the second day. On the third day, she began again to invent her stories and puns. Then she remarried.

And the sons of beautiful Egypt had another father.

After all, they'd given a beautiful burial to the dead father, they'd cried over him for the necessary time; buried him in a large white mosque that the Rayyis had had constructed during his lifetime, like his Pyramid. However, they lifted him out of his casket like any other Moslem; they placed him on the ground to make what is earth return to earth: so says Koranic law. Popular rumor recounted that the sewers near his mausoleum overflowed and fouled his body. But the news was denied.

Another rumor claimed that two angels went and visited him in his tomb: Munkar and Nakir. They questioned him about the Prophet. The dead man said:

"The Prophet, the Pastor, made himself shepherd of his people."

"And you?" Munkar and Nakir asked him.

Sadat, whose first name, Anouar, means "the brightest," took over power. A new father, new hope. Public rumor was not long in denouncing the change.

"What direction should we go?" a taxi driver asked of the new hope.

"Let's see here a bit ... In what direction was Nasser going?"

"To the left, Mister President," said the taxi driver.

"So go to the right," said the new hope.

A strange thing—this man who was going toward the right asked Hussein to be part of his cabinet, as Undersecretary of State in the Ministry of Culture, with the label of "Communist without a party!"

The prisons emptied out. Everything went well for a time.

Fakhr-el-Nissa was delighted about her brother's new position. He was going to encourage artists, guarantee their social status, permit big exhibitions. Layla hoped that the sacred theater would see the light of day, that bad TV programs would disappear and an authentic lifestyle and urban architecture adapted to the country would be sought out. Many projects were begun, and then stopped because of administrative weight and the rapaciousness of certain people.

But optimism about proper governance was quickly exhausted. The social and political situation was stagnating. The desert mirage continued to scoff at everyone. They ground their teeth. At the university, young people who had ambition and were refusing to become civil service retirees at age twenty dreamed once again of leaving, or despaired of living.

The chess game continued at a standstill, and the people attended the theater of pawns, rooks, queens and bishops, all pretending to devour each other with exhausted gestures. They were waiting and doing their daily prayers. Nothing was moving.

In May of 1971, Egypt had a ministerial reorganization. Hussein was on an official mission in Russia. He learned that the Communists in the resigning government were imprisoned. As he was preparing to return to France, it was announced to him, to his great surprise, that he'd been named Minister of Justice. "A hard-liner," said the press. Hard-liners were needed. Hussein, who played his reed pipe during his free time, missed the Ministry of Culture.

Layla's situation at the university became more and more difficult. Her students, angered at not seeing a future for themselves, believed that all men of power were donkeys. She saw Hussein dragging his desire to change the order of things like a cross. Once again, she went against the tide: she defended the men in power; without emphasis, without passion, with a bit of humor and all the bitterness she felt for having apparently been on the side of the privileged.

Yesterday, they were all twenty years old; they were dreaming of new values. Yesterday. Now they were living these sad tomorrows.

Why did the students take so many liberties with Layla? They had never been disrespectful. They simply liked to sit around her in a circle between classes and make her laugh. It was because she always had the time to listen. They said the men in power spent their time braying. War, peace, victory, liberty; they're just words, noisy words.

Layla observed that it took a lot of intelligence to speak of war and not make it; and even more to recognize that the people of Egypt were not talented in war. But youths wanted to throw themselves into the water in order to escape being smothered. They'd been promised that 1971 would be a decisive year for the fate of the Middle East. But November arrived, and it was still the status quo. Then December. Was it officially decreed that the year would have twenty-four months?

Layla's students knew why they wanted to fight: to recover their land and a future. They were afraid of nothing.

For some time already, people had been circulating again in darkened streets. War was predicted for the birthday of the Prophet, or for any propitious moment. The hopes for a negotiated peace died. The Israelis were powerful; they needed the land they were occupying. Children suffering from unemployment found makeshift work! A pot of blue paint in hand, they painted over car lights, pocketed a little piastre. A little farther on at a red light, another child, with an agile movement of his hand, wiped off the fresh paint. At the end of the evening they shared a meager pittance, enough to subsist, to be happy!

It was said that the people didn't believe in the Russians. It was said that in order to occupy Egypt, they were sinking her further and further into the mud, demanding all of her cotton. It was said that the Russians sent their planes with all the parts, but they systematically forgot one: for example, the wheels. It was said that one could at least sell a can of sardines to the Yankees at double the price.

Many students were in the army. Others demonstrated. They spent a night on Liberation Square, in front of the Hilton, built on the site of the English army barracks. The police clubbed, like everywhere; the students threw stones.

Public rumor didn't believe in the war. The Egyptians, they

said, fought like the people of Damiette:

"Let me tear him into pieces!"

"Don't stop me. I'm going to deal with him!"

"Make room so I can smash in his head!"

"Son of an assh …!"

"Son of a whor …!"

"Let go of my arm so I can beat him into a pulp!"

But the fist never hit, because the Damiette crowd knew its role well in the play being performed: firmly hold the combatants' arms and prevent them from coming to blows. The adversaries finished at the café, around a shisha. And when they returned home late at night, their wives covered them with caresses and admiration.

"My powerful bull," they said, as if they were pharaohs from times past!

A new National Committee of Workers and Students was formed, as in 1946. This time, the young army officers joined the movement. The bishops, the kings and the queens changed costumes. In the world of pawns, the son replaced the father. They were so alike that they tricked themselves.

The two giants pursued their game; their hands made a threatening shadow over the chessboard. The chess game was transformed into a game of massacre. What a roundup of pawns!

"And the pawns, those little pygmies, those idiots, they follow," said Layla. "Like donkeys. They're yelled at: 'Gee up! Shee! Haa! Gee! Ho!' They're whipped. They go right when they're beaten to the left, and left when they're beaten to the right."

"That's not true," said Hussein. "They walk straight. Straight toward the precipice."

Did Egypt die, once of fear and a second time of laughter? like the public wondered? No, beautiful Egypt is being choked: in southern Sudan, in Uganda, in Ethiopia, everywhere an Israeli presence. Israeli or American? Israel in the service of America or America in the service of Israel? In order to better surround Egypt, they looked for and armed Christians. They furnished them with military advisors. They took the side of the Southern Sudanese Christians against the Northern Moslems. They used Christian Ethiopia as a trampoline against Moslem Somalia and Eritrea. And the Russians wisely took the other side. American arms arrived in huge crates of medicine, sometimes stamped with a red cross.

One day, on the eve of spring in 1972, four wise black men would play mediator. The Israelis made promises and didn't keep them. The wise black men felt that they were being mocked because they were black. Uganda sent home its Israeli military advisors. The Northern Sudanese made peace with the Southern Sudanese. All over the world, Christians turned against power and took the side of the poor and oppressed of the earth. When the noose was loosened, they moaned a lot in the enemy camp.

Hussein played his role as Minister of Justice as well as could be expected.

During his youth, he wanted to change the world, fight against capitalism's inhuman face. The Egyptian-Russian friendship and the installation of a socialist regime delighted him: one day, capitalism would be defeated. He found himself, paralyzed by the shock, in a capitalist world without capital, where everything is bought and sold: honor, dignity, and integrity. He saw the rich man monopolize money and the poor man covet shiny money, protected money, far from those who need it, money that only gets along with money.

Minister of Justice! The words got stuck in his throat, choked him. Why not street sweeper? Brooms are more useful than these laws designed to be manipulated. Weight of the past, of hatred, of the propaganda machine, of the rules of the game, which keeps repeating itself. He joined a party in order to fulfill a dream from his youth. There he was, caught in the trap, in the gears of powerlessness.

He lacked neither faith nor hope. But he lacked power.

What would Hussein, Minister of Justice, do? He amused himself in committees, he laughed in public. One protects esprit de corps when one laughs. One works better. But he felt somber. He was delighted to be able to sleep so as to free himself and dream about proliferating brooms, like Ionesco's chairs, about amphibious brooms, like the Chitty-Chitty-Bang-Bang car, about flying brooms for monsters with big feet, and remote control brooms to cross borders and transform man. He spoke in his dreams. He was agitated, for hours, during nights of bad dreams.

Layla and Hussein stayed up. They drank a glass of *abarka*, the port of Coptic churches, or a glass of arrak, date alcohol from Saïd. They made vacation plans. Hussein was working too hard; they would run off to the desert, to the seaside. Alas! They'd still have to sweep away the armies who'd invaded all the beaches of the Mediterranean and the Red Sea. Or pretend not to see them? After all, in Suez, Israeli and Egyptian soldiers sometimes forgot they were there to fight. They looked at each other; they were bored. So they joked and laughed together. In Hourghada, some were Layla's or Hussein's students. They wore a gun on their shoulder in order to earn their meager salary. They'd be demobilized when they no longer knew what to do with them. The desert wasn't any less white, the sea any less transparent ...

In the spring of 1972, a choir of birds burst forth over the countryside. On the other side of the sea, the trees blossomed again, and nature was celebrating.

Near Rafah, they kicked out the Arabs. One third of the Gaza Strip emptied out. The following year, there would be room to house 75,000 Jews. The Arabs were still living in refugee camps. They were dependent on international charity. They dreamt of their houses, their lost lands. Some of them were given work, they were asked to construct the country of those occupying their land. The country was small. Not one day went by without the workers passing by the land that had once been theirs. Sometimes they killed. Because they were defeated, the reprisals were terrible. Houses were destroyed. Villages were destroyed.

In the spring of 1972, the birds sang, the trees bloomed again. North Vietnamese were found dead, chained to the seat of their tank. They had been told to fire on other Vietnamese from the South ... For many, the news didn't spoil the taste of coffee. For many, the day would be peaceful. However, a few thousand people demonstrated. Crazies, like Layla, who didn't understand the rules of the game, or who believed that peace had a chance, that men are too stupid to know how to seize it, and that the stupidest are those who make the pawns on the chessboard move, the Grands Guignols[1] of the earth!

In the spring of 1972, the trees were in bloom again, and men were still making war on each other ... it was said, on the sly, that the Russians, through the intermediary of Romania, were giving spare parts to the Israelis to allow them to use their 1967 booty, Stalin tanks in particular.

"We want to understand," cried out Layla's students. "It concerns our lives, after all!"

"Understand? It's complicated," said the newspapers; "but we'll try to explain. You have to first learn the rules of the game. It has nothing to do with your lives: there's money, there's oil, and there are political parties. These are the basic principles of the strategy. Never lose sight of them."

In May of 1972, a Khamsin wind swept through Cairo. Lily of the valley was growing on the other side of the sea. One morning, Fakhr-el-Nissa awoke, opened the window, and found the royal poincianas covered with red flowers. She began feverishly to paint red, fire, and joy.

The North Vietnamese defensive was a success: people who know how to fight better than the Egyptians; the President of the United States became crazy with rage. So much insolence from a group of Pygmies! He had the ports mined; he intensified the bombings ... On the political chessboard, the President of the United States took the place of a bishop. He moved diagonally, straight ahead.

A suffocating Khamsin wind was blowing over Cairo. Lilacs were flowering on the other side of the sea. Layla wanted to watch the game and laugh. She couldn't.

Hussein was busy bringing Egypt out of the impasse. There were council meetings that lasted until the morning, commission and sub-commission meetings late into the night. The contact with his colleagues made him forget his fantasies. Those ministers amused

[1] Les Grands Guignols: literally means "big clowns," but here refers to state terrorists.

themselves greatly, and they worked like madmen.

"We've never had such a good team," said Hussein. "Just look at your grandfather with his thick eyebrows, his big moustaches and his medals. In the past, one could recognize a minister by his suit. Today we're recognized by our laughter."

"All the same, you and my grandfather still resemble each other," retorted Layla. "Both of you are collaborating with a great power."

"Don't worry. The Russians are irritating you, they occupy the country, but their presence protects you. Your grandfather was a man of integrity. We need a lot of men like him."

However, Hussein decided to place all his bets on the Reds no longer. The game was worth it: convert to capitalism with the soul of a Communist; open the door to peace by giving one's luck to another great power, guarantee the capital needed for men to work; put it in the service of the people; lubricate the gears. He'd lived the Communist utopia. He'd seen the world divided between equally dishonest capitalists and revolutionaries, all ready to make war by using other people. He'd seen the rich of poor countries, from whatever political party, share the benefits of war. For Egypt, it was perhaps the hour of the Americans.

The Russians left after having almost officially exchanged gifts with the Egyptians: icons for pyramids. They left, accompanied by a tear from those who had profited from their presence, and followed by a dry eye on the part of those people in the street who'd always looked on them with suspicion; followed by the eye which delighted in seeing the formerly requisitioned buildings empty out: who would then profit from good old rents?

Layla and Hussein finally took the vacation they so desired at the Red Sea. Ferdous had just bought a lovely piece of land near the ocean; she'd had a simple house, like those of the fishermen, built. For the house warming, she had a sheep killed on the threshold of the door; she dipped her hand into the blood and made an imprint on the wall.

Khidr, the old fisherman's son, was getting married. He worked well: responsible for providing the army with fish, he earned twenty-two pounds per month. His fiancée was just a little girl, a cousin whom he'd never seen.

"Does a fisherman see the fish before fishing it?" asked the malicious old father.

However, she lived close by since she'd arrived with her family for the marriage. Everything had been done by letter. They cheated a little about the girl's age; they said she was sixteen in order to appease the public officials. Khidr's mother prepared a pretty trousseau with the money from the dowry: flowered cotton dresses, a Koran and a gold chain, the bedroom furniture ... She was happy to welcome a new daughter into her house.

Khidr and the child were awaiting the full moon to marry. They could have moved up the date of the ceremony, because there was electricity in the village, but tradition demanded that they marry at the full moon.

On the wedding day, they wouldn't show the handkerchief soaked with blood.

"Those are outdated customs," said Khidr's mother.

Layla and Hussein returned to Cairo with a treasure of songs learned from Khidr:

Put stone upon stone and begin again.
Go away, young man, I am engaged to the moon.
Moon! Allow me to rest in the light of your eye!

They hummed their songs in the busy streets or on the banks of the Nile, always listening for snatches of conversation on their way. In the *feshaoui* café, the tripe merchant from times past who was already serving revolutionaries back in 1919, two men were smoking the narghile. One said to the other:

"You're not married and you regret it! So think of all those people who envy you. In the past, you came home and found a patient wife; she didn't ask any questions; she took off your shoes, washed you, massaged you, and offered you nuts, syrup, cakes. Full of respect, she sat at your feet listening to you speak without interrupting, without looking up. Today, she wants to equal man; she puffs out her throat like a rooster at dawn, she cries out, she protests!

You return home in a peaceful mood, and there she is giving you enough of a headache to make you fall over stone dead. Listen to my advice: stay unmarried. As for me, I swear to you by the Prophet that one woman is already too much!"

In Sahara City, they ran into their neighbor, the butcher, who had married off his daughter. They congratulated him, had their picture taken with him, happy to fraternize with their butcher! They rediscovered the characters they'd always loved: the orchestra musicians resembling Saïdy peasants; the boys from Abu-el-Gheit who turn and whirl with their long hair, and who say that whirling dervishes still exist and that their mysticism is explained in books; and the belly dancers who seem to be part of the family life of the butcher or the scrap merchant. Was the belly dance ever erotic? And was the storyteller, accompanied by the grainy nasal sound of the rebab, ever poetic? In Sahara City, he improvised songs to the glory of Arab heads of state, and discreetly banked the money of their representatives in Cairo. Two black women with the profile of Akhenaten, a lanky black man, his torso decorated with a big necklace, bodies twisting in all directions, danced with fire. They too were Egyptians. They came from the far borders of the South, almost from Sudan.

Hussein and Layla were happy. They had once again found lost youth, laughter and a carefree attitude.

Layla told the story of the myth of the drunken Sekhmet; Sekhmet the lioness, goddess of war, transformed into a goddess of love:

"The god Râ sent her to earth to punish men. She massacred, killed, massacred, and devoured flesh and blood. Then the god Râ felt pity for men:

'They're not so bad,' said Râ.

'They have to be saved,' ordered the gods.

"And Râ decided to spread beer, colored with the red ochre of Assouan, over the entire earth. When she awoke, Sekhmet saw only blood. She gluttonously drank it, got drunk, and became the goddess of love. She was called Sekhmet-Hathor."

But in the month of November hope sank again. The Pales-
survivors of another September, which they called "black," too.
Israeli athletes hostage. The feelings of helplessness were general—
an ambush was arranged for the desperate men. Everything was lost
for them, so they killed and were killed. Anyway, they'd been dead
for three generations.

Great funerals were held in Germany for the dead Israelis. In
Libya, great funerals were held for the dead Palestinians. No one
thought of holding a common funeral for the victims of the same
tragedy.

And the reprisal raids began again. On Lebanon, this time;
Lebanon's water was necessary for Israel … Peasants and refugees
were massacred. Children were burned alive. Tanks crushed civilians.
Men took sides. Like the moon turning a light face to one part of
the earth, and a dark face to the other, like Janus Bifrons who wears
two faces, the good and the bad, so appeared the Palestinians and
the Israelis. The newspapers explained and condemned in a tone of
moralizing superiority. In Europe, it was said that the antagonism
between Jews and Arabs imposed new borders and that the West
would help Israel to define them. It was forgotten that in hatred
there are no safe borders.

Public opinion, turned away from the Vietnamese drama, was
busy judging the possessed, the desperate … spitting on them, those
hateful barbarians, those troublemakers, and those fanatic assassins.

In Cairo, people were afraid of reprisal raids. Egypt, crushed by
the weight of the masses, found the burden of war too heavy. She
had only one wish: to live, because she was afraid of becoming a
dead body, a smashed country that one day experienced convulsive
jolts, she wished to defeat the domination of money, she who saw at
her door and in her home, Money, always Money, crowned, coveted. Russia's ghost was no longer there pretending to protect Egypt.

Hussein's nightmares changed. The memory of his father burst
forth, hallucinating, from his deepest self; a body emptied by a slow
death, a long agony; a face with traits similar to those of an ancient
Egyptian mummy. His country, a dead body, perhaps, like that of

his father, that of Osiris, waiting for a criminal hand to dismember it. Piercing cries, wild dances and lacerated faces splattered with dirt inhabited his nightmares. His father and his country becoming one in the night. He awoke feeling bitter, feeling pain.

But no one can harm Egypt. Egypt is eternal! A nightmare is meant to end.

Hussein and Layla no longer hummed Khidr's song. Hussein played the pipe in order to fall asleep. But sad sounds no longer consoled him. Deaf despair accompanied him. For centuries, Egypt had resembled Osiris, the god of the dead. Throughout history, a new life had always burst forth. Would a new life again come out of the black hole, out of despair, out of death?

One black September morning Hussein was brought home on a stretcher. A thrombosis had felled him. He died with just enough time to say: "It hurts."

The official burial was simple, without pomp, without a cannon shot. The coffin, topped with a stele wearing a turban, and held up by big sticks to imitate a lion's paws, resembled a sphinx. Hussein's coffin was carried on shoulders all the way to the train station. Many unknown people crept into the procession to see up close the people in power accompanying it. Layla and Fakr-el-Nissa, dressed in black, their faces veiled, followed in a car, then by train. They buried Hussein in Minieh, in the neighborhood of Hoda Sha'araoui's tomb, the grand lady, in the same hole as his father, under a stele—karkûr, shhaid— a witness engraved with a name.

Layla's pain was great, as was her loneliness. But her eyes remained dry. She had lost the sense of reality. Her life became a sleepwalker's dream. Hallucinating images went by: all those she'd loved with Hussein and who had always said to her: there is nothing definitive about death; it always comes full circle with life. She remembered the years in prison, her past loneliness; Hussein wanted to change the world, renew the quality of life. Why did everything end in failure?

Layla would like to have written a little epitaph: "He lived among men in power, in fear of the powerful and the earth's disinherited; like the beautiful fish of the Red Sea who, in order to escape the sharks and the barracudas, jump out of the water and are grabbed by a seagull."

But she wrote nothing. Her gestures no longer followed her thoughts. She hardened herself so as not to feel self-pity.

She looked for refuge in myths, in the eternal past they had loved. The gardens of Osiris she had always planted for the Coptic Christmas were modest—barley and wheat in low vases—but she asked for a message from them. She scrutinized the bas-reliefs of temples, the papyrus vignettes of Anhaï and Hunefer. She deciphered hieroglyphics with a seer's sensitivity. *The Book of the Dead*: why did they call it that? The Ancients said: the Exit into the Day. Death was merely a setting sun. Vines, barley, wheat, cedar, all good pure things grew on Osiris's body.

Osiris nourished himself on wine, beer, all good pure things. He was buried in cedar. The coffin floated toward the North, all the way to Babylos, in Phoenicia. Osiris was lost in the celestial abyss, a starry body of the beautiful Nout, who would give birth to him; or on earth, the fertile cow Meh-ru: she carried in her an eye, a sun that would come out during the day.

Would Hussein return like the sun, barley, and wheat? Hussein was dead; he became a living Osiris. He passed man's limits. He metamorphosed into a plant, an animal; he was a lotus, a ram. He became multiple; he was all the gods. He killed evil, the snake Apophis. Peaceful, he became a peasant again; he labored, he cut down wheat, he seeded the fields of Ialou.

The body of "vegetating Osiris" lived in Layla's heart.

October 1973. It was war again, but it was out of the ordinary and overwhelming.

This time the Egyptian army took the initiative, and the surprise effect succeeded because the enemy had forgotten to count on the explosive force carried within despair. Engineers silently crossed the canal by boat; they leveled the damaged earth to allow tanks to pass, whereas on the other bank they threw up bridges. The air force unceasingly bombed Israeli defense positions. In the evening, the Bar-Lev line was occupied by the Egyptians. It took only a few hours to demolish a monster armed to the teeth, swollen with napalm. Pain and humiliation are slow to give way to joy. People walked in the streets, their transistor radios glued to their ears; in the salons, the announcers' voices from all the radios replaced conversation; they fed themselves on military communiqués: Syria attacked on the Golan front; the Egyptian army held its positions, three, four, five days. Six! The fateful number of 1967, which gave the Jew the illusion of Genesis repeated, that number was surpassed. A huge tank battle went on in the Sinai. On the Golan front, Syria battled hard. Would Jordan also open a front? Synchronized, the other Arab states entered into the battle. Oil threatened to flow no longer; the earth trembled.

Yehia again developed a taste for life by throwing himself into the hell of the Sinai.

Layla's servant carried his food, his clothes and his weaponry with him: everything he needed to live or die; there was nothing but fire before him. He no longer knew whether he was fasting or not fasting. He didn't have time to eat; death was hot on his heels. In the past he'd said: Allah! Allah! Allah! There was no longer time for mystical ecstasy. He repeated with the others: Allah Akbar! Allah is the greatest! If it were a holy war, perhaps he would never be able to fast again in his life; neither Ragab nor Ramadan; all of his false testimonies would be pardoned. But he didn't believe in holy war. He thought rather: a just war. However, he didn't like war. He no longer thought. He dreamed of laziness and the sweet joys of Ramadan evenings, of the lights of Sayeda Zeinab Mouled.

In Bar-Lev, he saw the enemy flee, barefoot like him in 1967. He wanted to laugh and to cry. He had taken the Jew for a warrior! He was just a man, like himself.

In Cairo, the evolution was strange. Silent, the cars circled in an orderly manner and stopped at red lights: an ambulance or army reinforcements might need to pass through. A spontaneous civic sense burst forth from all classes of society. Even the heavy bureaucracy awoke from its thousand-year sleep and began to be efficient. People looked with surprise at Sadat's picture. He was now a hero, prophet, and savior. During all these years he had thus acted like the scarab. He'd slowly crumbled the gamousse dung in a big pile, threatened to smother his earth. He'd taken a little pile; he'd laid his eggs in it, and he'd rolled his ball in front of him, slowly, surely. He'd buried it. One morning new life burst forth and the excrement changed into fertilizer. The people listened to a name, looked at a portrait and wondered how Sadat was modestly preparing, with a poisoned heritage, what Nasser hadn't succeeded in doing: Arab unity, but also national unity. Was a State thus going to efficiently put itself into the service of a people?

The people settled into peace. It was a peace filled with threats, certainly, a precarious peace. But the people threw themselves into peace with all the ardor of the ram in ancient times. They reconciled themselves with the West they had always loved. They were waiting for capital; they were waiting for money, work and the future. They anchored themselves in a brighter hope than the despair they had felt. They had not yet tasted the despair of the well-to-do. The people wanted to take a big bite of peace. Death? That was the past!

And Layla, would she ever begin a new life?

Glossary

Ades: Name of a Jewish family-owned department store.

Afreet: A ghost or ghoul; a humorous trouble-making spirit.

Akhenaten: Pharaoh of the XVIIIth dynasty who is considered, incorrectly, to be the founder of monotheism.

Al-Qarafa: The Moslem cemetery.

Amon: God of Thebes whose name means the "Hidden One."

Ashâsh: A train that stops at all villages.

Aton: The deified sun's disc.

Bakhoum: Name of a monk.

Betaoui: Bread.

Bey: An Ottoman rank below pasha.

Boab: Building caretaker; concierge.

Cham-el-Nessim: "Inhale the breeze." Ancient Egyptian spring festival that is celebrated on Easter Monday.

Chaouiche: A sergeant.

Chemla: Name of a Jewish family-owned department store.

Dabka: A Syrian dance.

Dallalah: A woman who does errands for others.

Djizzia: Money paid by a non-Moslem in a Moslem country for not serving in the army. A practice no longer in place in Egypt.

Eid-el-Kebir: The feast of sacrifice at the beginning of the pilgrimage to Mecca.

Feddan: A measure of land similar to that of an acre; five feddan equal two hectares.

Fellah: An Egyptian peasant. Plural: *Fellaheen*.

Foul medammes: Broad beans.

Furtwaengler: A famous German orchestra conductor.

Galabiyya: A robe-like piece of clothing for men and women.

Gamila: The Egyptian spelling of the name Jamila; the sound is a hard "g" in the Egyptian dialect.

Gezireh: The island where the residential neighborhood of Zamalek is located.

Ghorza: Hashish den.

Gueb: A god of ancient Egypt who represents the earth.

Hashâsh: A person who regularly smokes hashish.

Haschâschin: Plural of ashâsh.

Hagg: A person becomes hagg after a pilgrimage to Mecca.

Iftar: End of the fasting of Ramadan.

Jihad: Holy War.

Kanater-el-Qahira: Dams north of Cairo, built in the 18th century.

Karkûr: Stele.

Khamsin: The wind bringing desert sand and which creates immense sandstorms; the "sand wind." The name means "fifty" because it usually blows the fifty days between Easter and Pentecost.

Khawaga: A foreign man.

Khidr: Sufi wise man at the time of Moses.

Kholkhal: Ankle bracelet worn by a Bedouin or a peasant woman.

Mashrabeyya: Wooden latticework on a balcony that allows one to look out but not be seen by passersby.

Ma'taf: Storage basket for food.

Mawal: An improvised song with an emotional topic.

Meshanna: A platter made of straw, used most often for carrying bread.

Mohallel: A man paid to be a "temporary husband" so that a couple can remarry after a divorce.

Nabbout: A walking stick or stick for self-protection.

Nout: A goddess of ancient Egypt who represents the sky.

Offa: Hand woven basket.

Oke: Equals two *rotolis*, or 1,248 grams.

'Omdeh: Mayor.

Ragab: In the Islamic calendar, month preceding Ramadan.

Ramleh: In Alexandria, a seaside neighborhood.

Rotoli (or *ratl*): Equals one pound in weight.

*Saqui*ah: Mill powered by a cow walking round and round.

Shisha: Water pipe.

Sobek: A crocodile god.

Talaris: Change equaling twenty piasters (one-hundredth of an Egyptian pound). A piaster is equivalent to approximately one third of a U.S. cent.

Wafd: The political party that demanded Egyptian independence from Britain.

"*Wahaoui, ya wahaoui*": Refrain from a song sung by children to the moon during Ramadan.

"*Ya Moustapha, ya Moustapha Wana bahebak...*" Oh, Moustapha, oh Moustapha, and I love you."

Zabbal: Refuse collector.

Zaghareets: Ululation as an expression of joy.

Zamalek: A residential neighborhood of Cairo.

Zikr: "Remembrance." A remembrance of God by repeating his name over and over again; a Soufi practice.